THE COURT OF THE STONE CHILDREN

"When lonely Nina Harmsworth, newcomer to San Francisco, encounters lovely, mysterious Dominique in Mam'zelle Henry's private French Museum, she senses—but does not immediately comprehend—that customary time barriers have been broached. Impelled by her fascination with Dominique, who she gradually realizes lived in France more than a century before, Nina becomes involved in unraveling a generations-old mystery. . . . A gentle yet compelling story."   —*Horn Book*

"The author's highly imaginative integration of such diverse elements as childhood adjustment, concepts of time, prophetic dreams, mystery, and fantasy is ultimately successful and undoubtedly thought-provoking."
                                    —ALA *Booklist*, starred review

The Court of the Stone Children

THE COURT OF THE STONE CHILDREN

by Eleanor Cameron

PUFFIN BOOKS

PUFFIN BOOKS
A Division of Penguin Books USA Inc.
375 Hudson Street, New York, New York 10014
Penguin Books Ltd, 27 Wrights Lane, London W8 5TZ, England
Penguin Books Australia Ltd, Ringwood, Victoria, Australia
Penguin Books Canada Ltd, 10 Alcorn Avenue, Toronto, Ontario, Canada M4V 3B2
Penguin Books (N.Z.) Ltd, 182–190 Wairau Road, Auckland 10, New Zealand

Penguin Books Ltd, Registered Offices: Harmondsworth, Middlesex, England

First published in the United States of America by E.P. Dutton,
a division of Penguin Books USA Inc., 1973
Published in Puffin Books, 1990
7 9 10 8 6
Copyright © Eleanor Cameron, 1973
All rights reserved

LIBRARY OF CONGRESS CATALOGING IN PUBLICATION DATA
Cameron, Eleanor, 1942–   The court of the stone children/by Eleanor Cameron.   p.   cm.
"First published in the United States by Dutton in 1973"—T.p. verso.
Summary: Aided by the journal of a young woman who lived in
nineteenth-century France, Nina solves a murder mystery dormant
since the time of Napoleon.
ISBN 0-14-034289-3
[1. Space and time—Fiction.   2. Mystery and detective stories.]   I. Title.
PZ7.C143Co   1990   [Fic]—dc20   89–36035

Printed in the United States of America
Set in Janson

For Rita
and for Steve
who have a fondness
for fantasy

From the dark horizon of my future a sort of slow, persistent breeze had been blowing toward me, all my life long, from the years that were to come. —ALBERT CAMUS

The past is not dead; it is not even past. —WILLIAM FAULKNER

Our dreams are a second life. —GERARD DE NERVAL

Chapter One

They were standing in a group under the trees tossing
up wishes for the future, wishes and predictions, grand
and wild and inflated, boys and girls alike, but Nina, lost
in her own musings, wasn't taking it like that. "I think,"
she said seriously during a pause in the hubbub, "that
I'm going to be something in a museum. Yes," she
said, innocent and reflective, "yes, in fact I know I am,"
and they were convulsed. "I mean—" she shouted, "you
know what I mean," and wouldn't have cared, and
would have laughed with the rest at this joke on herself
if she could have felt she was one of them, if she could
have felt they'd accepted her as one.

"Something in a museum!" shrieked Marnychuck,
the first always to catch at any double meaning and make
use of it. "But you already are—you already are!" Little
and lean Marion Charles was, the girl they called Marnychuck, a person everybody turned to if there was some
plan afoot, some secret to be told, some piece of gossip:
Marny with her ironic self-assurance, her air of amused
knowingness.

Nina ran up the curving asphalt path that led through this small neighborhood park right to the top where there waited a tremendous view of the Golden Gate and a bench from which to absorb it. Stretched on his back, gazing up through leaves at the sky, one long leg draped over the other, his loose-leaf binder collapsed on his stomach, lay the boy she'd seen here before on her roundabout way home from school. He had his thumb in his binder keeping his place, and he had his pen, so he'd been writing. But probably not homework because his books were spilled across the grass. He turned his head and surveyed her without smiling, looking up catercornered from under a coppery thatch, and she turned and stared down at the others below, just visible through the branches.

"Well, I *am* going to be something in a museum! Some*one*! I *will* be. A—" But it was gone, clean gone, the word that had hung in her mind just as she ran up the path, so that she'd felt, for a second or two, secure.

Not to her—more to himself, "A curator," the boy said.

"Yes, a curator," she shouted down. "That's it—a curator."

But Marny and her friends couldn't have cared less about museums and curators. They turned; they moved off in a straggling line along the lower path, and the girls were all going to Marnychuck's because her mother worked and they could do as they pleased, turn up the radio full blast, laugh, scream, eat, until Marny cleared them all out just before her mother got home. Nina had never any hope of being invited. She was too new; she understood that.

"Still too new, Nina, after four months?" Why did her mother keep harping away about it? Being new wasn't the trouble.

"Well, where're all the hordes of new friends you and Dad've been making?"

"But you're young, Nina. You're not occupied. You have time. At your age it's always easier to make friends than at Dad's and mine."

Nina saw no sense to this and didn't believe it. In fact she'd been moved to think lately that at her age everything to do with people must surely be more difficult than at any other. And she didn't want, really, to be invited to Marnychuck's, with the strain it would have meant of being constantly on her guard against saying something innocent and foolish, but above all against Marny, impervious as a crocodile and no doubt born as shrewd as one. No, what Nina was most passionately convinced of was that she wanted nothing of this ugly city—nothing at all. She wanted just to go back home, back up to Silverspring in the foothills of the Sierra Nevadas where she had lived her whole life and where her real friends were—Laura, the daughter of Mrs. Bourne, who had charge of the little Silverspring National Monument, and the Hudson twins, Maizie and Rupe, who were taking care of her cat Windy. Oh, she knew lots of other kids up there, but these were the ones who counted. These were the ones she missed.

"But this is home, Squirrel," her father would say, and he'd watch her face, smiling a little as if in encouragement, yet with something anxious lurking in his eyes. "Not this apartment, but San Francisco. We'll find a place." Yet no real effort was being made, no constant,

[3]

steady effort on weekends, which was the only way it could be done. And they'd never find one—*never*. She knew that now. He had said it so many times about finding another place that it was unbearable and she felt embarrassed for him because of the special way she felt about him. Her throat ached whenever they spoke of it. Her stomach tightened.

She followed Marnychuck and the rest of them with her eyes until they disappeared, and after a little, while the sparrows cried "cheep, cheep" in the underbrush like mechanical birds and the sounds of traffic came up from below,

"Why do you want to be a curator?" the boy asked. "Women *can*, I suppose. I mean, there's no law against it—only it's queer you should think of it. Of course there's Mam'zelle, but then she owns the whole place."

As a matter of fact, Nina too thought it queer she should have said what she had, about wanting to be something in a museum. It had never really occurred to her before as far as the future was concerned, despite the fact that she'd worked after school and weekends in the little Silverspring National Monument for Mrs. Bourne, helping to sweep and dust, file cards and type labels and even do some of the arranging. Other times she'd had the idea of being a veterinarian or maybe a forest ranger if a woman ever could.

She turned to the boy, who was still studying her with eyes of the most intense blue she had ever seen, apparently wanting to know just why she had this unlikely notion, and Nina went over and sat down on the bench and looked straight at him. "I'd never been in a real museum," she said, "not a big one, until we came to San Francisco. And when we went into the one over in the park—" She stopped, searching for the exact right words to make known the excitement she'd felt. "The building was so huge, with all those rooms keeping on opening out, I thought I'd never come to the end. And there were so many millions of things to see—" She hesitated, shyness holding her silent.

The boy smiled to himself as though thinking of something he had no intention of telling. "Did you go into the furnished rooms, like the ones in a castle or palace, or the big old medieval houses?" There was something oddly alert in the way he was watching her, waiting for whatever it was she would answer.

Her face lighted with astonishment. "But that's it— that's it!" It was as if he had read her thought, because it *was* the rooms that had held her longest, for some reason she could not have explained.

"I know." And the way he said it, she caught, with a curious quickening of the blood, an awareness of what he, too, must have imagined, the peculiar sensations he, too, might have experienced in those rooms with their massive pieces of furniture, carved, worn by thousands of hands, by innumerable brushings of cloth and flesh— all gone, gone long since. Blackish they were, mostly, crookedly made—benches, chairs, wardrobes, enormous chests, vast canopied beds. But whatever feelings the sight of those rooms had given her, whatever sense of the past, whatever wordless intimations, had been shattered again and again by her mother's, "Come *on*—come *on*, Nina. For heaven's sake, don't make us keep coming

[5]

back for you!" "But there's no *time*," Nina had raged. "You don't give me *time*—why can't you leave me and just go on!"

"In the mountains," she said to the boy, "up in the gold rush country where I come from around Silverspring, there're the ruins of one old gold rush town after another. I hate the made ghost towns, the ones they fix up—"

"The ratty old stuffed bodies," said the boy, "sitting inside stores and jails in the dark, and some with their legs hanging out of windows."

"Me and my friends," Nina said, "know where Hangtown is, and Dead Man's Hill and Lost Mine and Bloody Gulch. They're buried in weeds in the back country, but we found them. And I used to go off and pretend the towns were all still there the way they used to be and that I lived in one of the cabins and had gone for a walk. Out in the back country, it could be any century. And there're old tombstones, and you wouldn't believe how many there are for kids our age and for babies and little children two and three years old. It must have been so hard in those days just to get started living."

The boy sat up and again fixed her with those disturbing eyes of his.

"If I was to be so early done for,
    I wonder what I was begun for,"

he said softly. "But that isn't all there is to it. 'What lies on the edge of perception, from where anyone might come moving in?' My mother said that." And then, unexpectedly, he chuckled. He grinned to himself and sat

[6]

up in one neat, uninterrupted movement. "Lonny's all right. She goes on about stuff that doesn't matter like recipes and keeping some sort of order, but she knows things. I mean, she's really all *there*."

Nina stared at him. And it wasn't only his words, but a certain stillness and remoteness she could feel in him now as he seemed to turn over some sudden thought, that sent a ripple of uncertainty through her. She remembered his silences, his eerie watchfulness. There was something about him, no doubt emphasized by his coppery hair, that reminded her of a fox; perhaps it was the way he moved, quick and light. "But I don't understand—" she said.

He did not explain, for there came a threatening reverberation over to the north, and their heads lifted and turned like the heads of animals in a forest. Across the green-black waters of the bay, whipped here and there into whitecaps running before the wind, the bridge spanning the Golden Gate shone out an almost unearthly white, delicate at this distance, slung across space under the green and purple bellies of storm clouds moving in over Marin County. You could scarcely see the land, lost in a glimmering dimness over there on the far side—only that shining bridge. It was a sight you might hold in your mind for the rest of your life: that bridge hanging under clouds filled with an ominous black light. Yet where the boy and Nina sat the sun was still shining with the brilliance it had all day, only now a thin mist was beginning to sweep across its face and a freshet of damp wind began pushing at the undersides of leaves. The tops of trees were beginning to bend and whisper.

All at once the boy leaned down and scrabbled his

books together and heaped them on top of his binder. "Gotta go," he said, and stood up.

But there was something she had to ask him, something of urgent importance, because what if by some crazy chance she never had the courage to speak to him again? It could be all different next time, considering how queerly and abruptly people of her age changed toward one another—or how queerly he might change. "What was it you said? Something about a woman—" She sat looking up at him, her face full of an anxious effort to make clear what the connection had been. But his expression was blank. "*You* know!" she exclaimed. "You were saying how strange it was for me, a girl, to want to be a curator, and then you said—"

"Yes, Mam'zelle and the French Museum. See down there?" and she stood beside him while he pointed out over the steep, leafy street below them to where another street ran into it. And in what looked like a park, like this one only not hilly, Nina made out a long, pale yellow building—no, not yellow; more a pale gold it seemed in this brooding storm light—that stood in a sweep of lawns scattered with trees. "A woman owns it—Mam'zelle Henry. Actually, she's Mrs. Henry, but her gardener's always called her Mam'zelle since he worked for her family in France, so now everyone does. The museum's private, but it's a real museum and you can go in." He looked at his watch. "Twenty to four. It closes at five-thirty—you've got time."

Nina, knowing she would have to go, that she would have to chance it, thought of swollen clouds and her mother phoning. Calling out "Thanks!" she began running downhill toward that leafy street where she had

[8]

never been, toward the golden building, and it was as if she were back in the hills in Silverspring, up early in the morning before anyone else was awake, running and running as though she had no weight, nothing to hold her back, no unwilling flesh or pounding heart, a bodiless Nina filled with eagerness and joy. She felt now that she was racing toward an appointment, agreed upon and written down long ago in some forgotten or unknown moment. Presently she heard the thud of feet behind her and the boy caught up; they raced for a second or two and then he passed her, sending a glance of teasing, mocking challenge back over his shoulder. In another turn of the path he was gone and she said to herself, I'll never see him again, and what she meant was that they'd never talk again—not as they had just now, up at the top of the hill.

But when she came out of the park onto the street, there he was waiting for the signal to change. She stood beside him, catching her breath, at ease and feeling no need to speak. Then the signal went green and they crossed.

"Think I've been in that little museum up in Silverspring," he said.

"You *have*?" She was filled with surprised delight. She'd always felt it to be especially hers, every change, every new possession noted. It was in that modest building that she had first heard the word "curator."

"I love it," she said. "All the settlers' things, and the miners'—and seeing how small people used to be, the women's little shoes, and their waists. Why, I couldn't begin to fit. My shoes are clodhoppers. I'd say to my father, 'Just think, we can touch the real boards, and the tools and clothes and dishes they used all those years ago,' but Dad laughed at me because when he was a boy he was taken to the British Isles to see a place up in the Orkney Islands called Skara Brae where there's stone furniture underground that the Neolithic men put there. He says that was thousands of years ago, and the stones are still in place just the way they left them."

The boy stopped and she turned in surprise, and there he stood, his eyes fixed upon her with a steady, piercing intensity. "You said—what was the name of that place?" He even cocked his head a little as though to catch more than whatever it was she would answer.

"Skara Brae—"

"And where is it?"

"In the Orkney Islands, right up at the top of Scotland. Dad showed it to me on the map."

The boy's gaze continued, unwavering, and Nina was so preoccupied in trying to figure the reason for this that it never occurred to her to be embarrassed. Besides, he was looking right through her.

"I'll go there," he said presently, with the utmost conviction, and it was not even as if he were making himself a promise, for promises can be outmaneuvered by fate. No, he was simply stating a fact, a foregone conclusion. Then he looked away and they started walking again, their long legs getting into stride, and after a bit they came to the museum grounds.

"Why do you want to go to Skara Brae?" Nina asked. "And how did you know about my Museum Feeling?"

As though his mouth couldn't help itself, there was his little half-smile again. "Because of my project." Apparently this answer did for both questions, and the way he said it, the words came out with capitals and quotes, "My Project," as if he were speaking of something private he need never explain to anyone. But what Nina felt most keenly was that with this private preoccupation of his he could be secure unto himself forever and need not be envious of anyone as she herself had been disgustingly envious of Marnychuck. "Well, so long," he said, because here they were in front of the golden building, in front of the big pulled-open wrought iron gates where a wide avenue beckoned toward steps that led up onto a pillared loggia. She turned to him to say something—some last thing—but already he was off, and he never once gave a single glance back. He had a kind of springy lope that, now she had talked to him, seemed to her to express a contained eagerness at being alone again on the track of his own thought.

Chapter Two

The sun shone out, dazzling, so that the two-storied building with its wings at either end, sweep of lawns, trees and shrubbery, were flooded in brilliance, all deep green surfaces given a sheen. Yet thunder continued to grumble and growl over Marin County. And when Nina passed from sun to shade, an edge of wind touched her cheek, drew another veil of mist across the sun—then out it came again. Voices of leaves speaking together rose in volume as she advanced up the avenue toward the museum doors. She felt an expectancy in the air and in the silence that followed a sense of someone waiting.

I'm coming! But to whom did she call? She would have broken into a run if a woman's voice hadn't been heard at that instant.

"Lisabetta!" it cried. "Lisabetta!" in fond, teasing tones. "You silly cat—" As she spoke, a cream-colored cat with a tabby tail, tabby face, and tabby paws streaked across the walk in front of Nina, scrambled up a tree and down again. "It's the weather, Auguste—" *Oh-goost* was the way she said it, and Nina looked up to see a woman leaning out of a second-story window. "There'll be rain, you can depend upon it. Did you hear the thunder?" She broke into a torrent of energetic exclamations which Nina could not understand but which she took to be directions, for the woman was gesturing and pointing to various spots in the garden.

Then here came Auguste, bronzed, creased face topped by a snowy cap of hair, an old man in a faded shirt and with leather chaps over the fronts of his trouser legs. Now he leaned and swooped up Lisabetta as she came to him, and he grinned at Nina, sent her a wink over Lisabetta's back. "*Oui*, Mam'zelle!" he tossed up on a note of long-suffering patience, and one blunted old hand waved about over his head as though chasing off a fly. "*Oui—oui—absolument!*"

"*Mais*, Auguste—yesterday—"

"Hey, Ph'lippe," bawled Auguste toward the far corner of the shrubbery—a phone rang, the wind rose, there was a cry of sharp impatience as if at papers blowing, and the casement slammed. Auguste chuckled, and there was something wicked and pleased in his chuckle. "Ver-ry beautiful, *n'est-ce pas*? My little sweetheart?" At the look of astonishment on Nina's face, he chuckled again, wickeder than ever. "The cat, *p'tite*, the cat— Lisabetta. Not Mam'zelle! You ever seen a Si-tab? That's my Lisabetta, a Siamese tabby. My little queen."

Philippe appeared, a huge, shock-headed young man, over whom Auguste poured the flood of Mam'zelle's instructions. Nina went on up the steps onto the pillared loggia and pulled at the bronze knob of one of the tall double doors and entered the museum.

She was surrounded by vistas, by depths and airiness,

distances along green-golden halls that ended in enormous windows through which could be seen boughs moving in the sun and shadow. The whole place seemed mysteriously alive. She could hear footsteps, whispers and echoes and murmurings. She did not know which way to venture, for all points beckoned, so she revolved in a slow circle of enchantment in order to take in the full beauty of this lofty central hall paneled in honey-colored wood from which a flight of stairs curved to the second floor, a flight edged in a burnished filament of scrollwork and banister. Paintings hung against the paneling. The polished floor shone green-gold, stretching away and away. She was aware of someone sitting behind a desk on her left, but he or she seemed scarcely to exist as Nina stood bemused, looking, listening, soaking up the spirit of the place through skin and senses and nerves. After a time she was drawn to a particular painting hanging near the corridor on her right.

It was of a great fish, green and blue, and it had wings with red in them and it had a human arm which was, oddly enough, playing a little violin. Below the fish, the top slightly behind it, there swung—or at least rested in air—a pendulum clock; behind the fish and the clock was a blue sky, not pale, summery blue, but powerful evening blue, and beneath was a river and on the deep blue at the side a man and a woman lay, embracing. Nina couldn't get over the wonder and strangeness of this painting. It reminded her—of what? Of dreams; yes, it was as impossible and as full of meaning as dreams are, meanings you can't quite fathom and that recall long ago happenings you can't quite remember, happenings that haunt and hover, yet will not give up the whole of themselves.

"And what do you make of the painting?" asked a voice. Nina turned and saw a woman coming toward her, a woman who swayed through the bronze light like a dolphin through seawater. She had a mass of coiled-up hair, and two silver darts pierced the coil, Nina saw as the woman turned her head to look up at the picture. She was not the one of the upstairs window, who had been small and vigorous, but someone taller, calmer, quieter, with deep-set eyes.

"I don't know. I wish I knew what it meant. It's like a fairy tale—or a dream—"

"Yes, it is," exclaimed the woman as if surprised at Nina's perception. "You've hit it exactly, the precise quality of that painting. It's by Chagall and he called it *Time Is a River Without Banks.* If you try to make sense of it by means of logic, you can't, because Chagall is always remembering his childhood and so, probably, his childhood dreams, and the feeling of losing himself in fairy tales. Do you like it?"

"I wish I could have it," Nina said without a moment's hesitation. "*Time Is a River Without Banks,*" she repeated, and thought instantly of the boy. But why? Why should the painting make her think of him? When she saw him again she must ask him.

"May I help you?" the woman wanted to know. "Is there some special department—?"

"The rooms," Nina said. "Do you have rooms furnished from past centuries?"

"Oh, yes—we have many of them. This whole end

of the building." She pointed along the corridor.

And so it was. You could lose yourself drifting from one to another, as Nina now did, as though time were indeed a river without banks, "As though this is my home," she said, then looked to make sure no guard or visitor was nearby, "this French—what is it? Yes, my father's château, and these rooms are ours. That's his library, and over here, our small private dining room where we have just a few friends—not like that big one back there where we give dinners for ambassadors and things like that."

It was round, this little room, with walls of gray-green painted with fruits and flowers in panels and garlands picked out in gold. There were white statues standing in niches, and a mirror over the fireplace reflected the light, and shadows of leaves moving on the wall near the windows. Striped satin chairs stood about on a parquetry of golden brown wood set in patterns. A chandelier of crystal and tall candles was suspended over a round table set for four, its glossy cloth hanging in folds to the floor. "But, Nanette," said Nina, "you've forgotten the flowers for the center. I said yellow tulips. I always want flowers for the table—you know that." There were no ropes across the entranceways to doors, no signs on chairs, and Nina went in and walked leisurely to the long windows to tell Auguste that he must bring wood for the fire. "The guests will be here any minute—the fire should have been lit by now—"

She was at the window, looking across the lawn to a wooded grotto which she would certainly have to visit the next time she came. As she stood there, she felt someone behind her—and there it was: her Feeling, the sense of timelessness, an acute awareness of being freed of the moment. She held her breath, looked down at her own hand resting on the windowsill, and it seemed scarcely to belong to her. She looked at the shadows on the wall and they seemed not shadows any longer but living shapes of an indescribable beauty against color so deep as to invite her to enter it, as if it were no longer solid but some depthless medium in which she might become lost. The flowers and fruits were no longer painted, but hung there, giving out color like light, yet rounded and fluted and planed as if you might touch them and hold them. They had a fragrance, and Nina heard the stillness of this Moment piercing her brain in a tone beyond the pitch of sound. "No!" she said. "No!" for it was as though she stood on the brink of an abyss, and if she stepped forward, that step would be final.

The presence behind her waited; she could feel the waiting, and she too held still, listening for some move on the other's part, some rustle or footfall. She looked down, and the Moment was gone. Her hand was her own hand; the leaf shapes on the wall were shadows only; the fruits and flowers were painted, the silence had lost its eerie pitch and Nina heard voices in the corridor and the answer of the guard.

Her face went scarlet, for what could she say when she turned to that person who stood there? She had said "No!" twice, and before that had given directions out loud about the flowers and the wood. Yet whoever was there uttered no sound; there was nothing to be sensed now but a kind of breathing expectancy. Nina twisted round, smiling casually as if to herself over some secret joke. But there was no one. Whoever it had been had already moved on.

She went to the door and looked out. The hall was empty except for the guard, teetering from heel to toe with his hands behind his back down there at the end of the corridor near the big window, which was no longer filled with sun and shadow but with a steely blue light. Baffled, she went to the last room on the other side, smaller even than the little dining room and therefore evoking a greater feeling of coziness. It too was painted a soft gray-green with panels and garlands of flowers and with a golden brown floor set in patterns. There was a desk between the long windows on Nina's left, a dressing table opposite the door where she stood, and across from the windows on her right a closet bed built into a deep recess in the wall over which curtains could be drawn.

"My bedroom—"

She stepped forward, heard the thunder coming nearer, and in that instant turned her head and saw distinctly, etched in sharp bright and dark and sitting curled on the bed with her back to the wall and Lisabetta at her side, a girl of about her own age, who was regarding her with a look of sparkling interest and welcome. Lisabetta never moved, bunched up in a mound with her tail wrapped around herself, her head turned toward Nina and her gaze, too, steady and unblinking.

Lightning had crackled and vanished, and for the first time Nina realized how dark it had become. It was late! Now thunder rolled down and hit the sky directly above the roof of the museum. But Lisabetta never moved, nor the girl on the bed, and their gaze seemed not to shift from their contemplation of Nina. The girl's face, her hands and arms, and the cat's fur glimmered in the shadowy recess. Now it began to rain—faster and faster—a torrent, a deluge. The wind blew and beat the rain against the windows. It could not rain any harder and yet it did.

What time is it? Mother anxious, phoning. "I must—I must—" her mother would say. "We must always—you must always—" What must I always? Think of someone else besides myself.

"I knew you'd come," said the girl in a low voice. "There's plenty of time for us—for you and me. So you'd better go now." Then, after a second's silence, "You'd better hurry," she said with the utmost serenity, so that the word "hurry" came with indescribable strangeness from her, as though it could not possibly, even having been spoken, bear any relation to her. "I knew you'd come," she said again.

"But what do you mean!" exclaimed Nina. "*How* did you—?"

"It doesn't matter," came the reply. "Not now. You'd better go, but come back. Be sure to come back. Though of course you will. Of that we can be certain."

While she backed toward the door Nina kept her eyes on the girl, whose hand seemed to flicker over Lisabetta's head. Then she whirled and raced along the hall, and when she came to the central foyer, she ran to the desk where a dignified old gentleman sat reading a newspaper.

"The telephone—could I—?"

"By all means, child. By all means."

Mrs. Harmsworth was occupied with a customer, the woman in the bookstore said, as if any difficulty or desperation on Nina's part were of small importance. There followed some confusion, and then her mother spoke.

"Mother, I'm at the French Museum."

"Where in the name of heaven is *that*! It's five-thirty and absolutely pouring. I've been trying and trying to get you, Nina. What are you going to do? How are you to get home?"

"I don't know. I didn't think about time—there didn't seem to *be* any time. I could wait—"

"But the museum is closing now," reminded the elderly gentleman, leaning forward and rustling his paper, and as if in support, a bell sounded throughout the building, adding, for no sensible reason, to Nina's mood of desolation.

"I'll just come on home—*yes*, it's blocks and blocks. But maybe there's a cable car. Of *course* I'll be sopped—but the museum's *closing*—"

A hand was laid on her arm. "I have an extra umbrella," the woman's voice said. "Tell her not to worry—there's a cable car two blocks over."

When Nina hung up the receiver, "It's as if it's the end of the world, as if I'm a million miles from home and won't get there 'til midnight and kidnappers are in between. Or as if I'm about five years old in this big, wicked city." She took the proffered umbrella and gave the woman a quick little half-smile. "It's not me that's worried. What if I do get sopped? You know—" and she started to put up the umbrella then remembered she was still inside. People who had been in the back of the building and in the opposite wing from the furnished rooms were emerging from corridors, their footsteps echoing, and going out the big double doors. People were coming down the curved stairway from the upper floor, pausing to look at the paintings, murmuring to each other, crossing the foyer, and the doors opened and closed, opened and closed, and the sound of rain and the smell of soaked earth was blown in coldly in puffs and gusts. The sound was torrential.

"Yes?" urged the woman, her eyes resting on Nina with interest.

"I liked the girl," Nina said. "Is she your daughter? I liked her being on the bed in the little bedroom with Lisabetta by her, even though she scared the living heck out of me, especially because of the lightning. I'm afraid I wasn't very friendly, only I didn't see what she meant by saying she knew I'd come. Now that was peculiar. When I was running up the walk to the museum—" But how had it been? What exactly *had* she felt running up the walk to the museum?

"I don't know what you—" began the woman, and the telephone rang and the elderly gentleman answered, then held out the receiver.

"For you, Mrs. Staynes."

She took it without looking, her eyes still on Nina. "No, I can't imagine—" and then spoke absently into the mouthpiece.

Nina went over to the doors, out across the loggia, put up Mrs. Staynes's umbrella, and stepped into the blinding rain.

Chapter Three

In fifteen minutes, because she did not know this side of the park, because of dead ends, and because the heaviness of the downpour made it hard to lift the umbrella high enough to read street signs, Nina was lost.

It had been along the tree-lined street, the one at the foot of the park where the boy had stood waiting for her, that the cable car ran. But well before she could reach the corner she saw the cable car pulling away, as blackly laden with passengers as a honeypot with bees, so that there would have been no room for her in any case.

Now, instead of climbing back up into the park and going home the way she knew, she ran on under the heaving boughs of the trees, past the tall, tiered homes set behind brick walls in those clipped and tended gardens she had looked down on from the top of the park. Were these what you would call the mansions of the rich? They were fabulous, these tall separate homes in a city of apartment houses jammed tight against one another, homes with their big windows looking out into the park on one side and across the bay on the other. Large, perfectly kept cars drew up and turned in—Nina stopped, peering out from under the dripping edge of Mrs. Staynes's umbrella—while the master with his brief-case and folded newspaper leaned forward, gathering his possessions, and the chauffeur drove the car sleekly down the inclined drive. The garage door, untouched by human hands, rose as the car advanced, the interior lighted itself, the master got out, and the garage door went down.

She ran on, missed the street that turned off to the left around the park, and found herself in a business district of glaring, dirty shops she had never seen before. Trousered legs, lean, black with rain on the thighs, advanced and passed. Drenched skirts whipped back; old people in broken shoes and shapeless coats talked to themselves, clutched their bundles in dripping hands, their heads down and faces twisted against the knives of rain. A man swore at her when she butted blindly into his side. Once when the rain stopped for a little, she let the umbrella fall and stood at a street corner gazing up at sea gulls planing in circles in a patch of silver sky.

"Come on, come on, girl—you'll never get home that way!" An ancient dame, merry and toothless, her old head bare to the elements, grabbed Nina by the arm and swung her into the street, then on the other side skipped off lively as a sand flea and disappeared down an alley where garbage cans spilled their orange rinds and coffee grounds and stained papers onto the sidewalk.

Six-fifteen, said the staring electric clock, jerking from second to second on the streaked wall of a restaurant. People in there, in the cold, hard light, pushed food into their faces, never bothering to take the plates off their trays, and they still had their coats on, and their hunched shoulders were streaked with rain. The museum, the museum! The picture of it was in her mind, but especially now the little dining room with pale walls, the leaf shadows moving, the long windows with their draperies held back by cords, the feeling of enclosed delicacy and airiness.

She ran on, asking the way here, there, to her own street, but the replies she got in the downpour came muttered and indistinct. It was like being in a nightmare, where there is no possible way home and time stretches into infinity as if with some sly purpose.

Now someone pointed her to her own street, incredibly steep where cars were nosed in across the sidewalk, and with a sob of relief Nina ran up the dark steps she knew. And there was a man in the entryway taking a magazine from the hook under the Harmsworths' mailbox, and because of all that had happened, an unreasoning rage boiled through her. She raced up and snatched the magazine, and the man's mouth fell open.

"Thief!" she yelled at him in a fury. "It's ours—*ours*—" and pelted off down the hall, up the stairs, up another flight, and banged at her own door and wrenched it open.

But they were strangers who turned astonished faces to her under the harsh glare of an overhead light: a man, two women, a boy, and some little children, pudding faces with prunes for eyes and slits for mouths. They stared at her. One of the women scraped her chair back from the table set with steaming food. But nobody said anything, only gazed, only gawked, and the smell was of sauerkraut or brussels sprouts, and of burned fat.

Wordlessly Nina backed away, clapped the door closed, and stumbled off down the stairs. She knew—she knew! This building and the one next to it were identical. It was something she had found unendurable, that they were so exactly alike you could hardly tell them apart unless you lived in one of them. And she *did* live in one of them, and *could* recognize the difference, but in the rain had paid no attention. The man was on the stairs, fumbling his way up in the dim, anonymous gloom, and he was thin, rather frail, and again his mouth gaped open when she paused in her flight and shoved the magazine back into his hand. "I'm sorry," she cried. "I'm so sorry—" and leaped on down and left him standing there, whispering in mystification.

When she came to her own apartment, coldly she got her key out of her purse and unlocked and opened the door, then closed it and stood with her back against it. She was—not home, but where temporarily she had to come.

Her mother and father looked at her. Her mother was standing at the table by the window, and she had the curtain pulled back so that she must have been watching, and her father was in the easy chair under the lamp; he had no doubt been trying to read but his newspaper was on the floor at his feet. Nina saw his eyes close for a second and then he held out his arm. But she did not move, nor make any response.

"Where have you been, Nina—*where have you been*!" Her mother was coming toward her, but her father still said nothing, only held her with his eyes. "I've gone down to the front a hundred times—" Her mother's hands were on her shoulders, sliding down to her skirt, feeling the wet, taking Mrs. Staynes's umbrella so that it wouldn't make a pool on the rug. "Nina, you're so cold. You're shaking. You must have a bath—a good, hot bath—"

Shaking, yes, but not from cold. Nina stiffened, turned her face and pressed it against the door. "This city—I *despise* it. I won't stay. I'm going back to Silverspring. I'll live with the Hudsons. Maizie said I could before we left—"

Still her father said nothing, only she was aware of his steady gaze. His arm had dropped, but her mother's hands came up to her shoulders again, and she could feel the pressure.

"Nina, what happened? Did someone—did some man—?"

"No, no! Nothing like that," cried Nina impatiently. "I got lost, and it's all so ugly—so *ugly*!" She pushed her mother away and went across the living room to the narrow hall where there was a little blind kitchen, and next to that a blind bathroom and, at the end, the bedroom where her mother and father slept. She went into the bathroom and closed the door and locked it, and nobody came or said anything, but she could hear her mother on the other side of the wall moving pans around on the stove. Her father had sat silent in his chair. His fault, he'd no doubt been thinking, his fault for bringing them here, yet after the year of his illness with bills to pay and too little money, there being not enough business in a small place like Silverspring for two accountants so that he'd lost his clients in that year to someone else, what could he have done but come to the city when a job was offered? Nina wept furiously under the shower, mingling her tears with the shower water, pulling her straight dark hair back over her ears like a boy's, pressing it sleek as an otter's pelt. Fool, she called herself. Stupid ass, stupid fool to get lost and panic-stricken so close—not to home, *not ever home*.

She dried herself and slipped into the hall with her clothes held against her, and in the bedroom, in the dark, got into her pajamas and robe and slippers. Still in the dark, she went to the window and looked out through the rain to a narrow slit of lighted city, shining between the roofs of stores. "A crack of view," she said aloud, "a slit of view," and once she had looked across a blue valley to the mountains on the far side, furred in green, in thick forests. From the freeway that curves into San Francisco, she had seen street after street lined solid with the straight fronts of buildings like this one, standing flat against one another, hillsides of them, mile upon mile of them, going up and down, like thousands and thousands of different colored dominoes. And she would never have imagined, until she saw it, that people could exist without the sight of green through their windows, without sky, sometimes with nothing but a wall.

Someone came to the bedroom door, and by his step she knew it to be her father. He came over and his arms went around her; his chin rested on the top of her head. "We'll find a place," he said. "Don't you worry, Squirrel, we'll find one—some little house."

Some little house! How lightly he said it, how carelessly, the way he always did. He was like a child, saying over and over words that meant nothing.

"How can we?" demanded Nina, her throat tight and burning so that the question could scarcely get through. "What is there to find that we'd want? A *house!*" And she meant that for people like themselves, with no car (their last, just before they came from Silverspring, hadn't been worth keeping), in a city like this where there was not a house they could afford to rent except miles and miles out, there could be only more apartments. What they *had* to find, Nina kept saying, was some sort of special apartment, with a view of trees.

"Squirrel, Squirrel, you're like a bonfire, blazing and crackling. Your fury never dies down—"

"But it can't, it can't," and she twisted round to face him. "Dad, don't *let* this place do. Don't get *used* to it. Hate it—*keep* hating it! It's the only way out."

"You're cruel, Nina," her mother would say to her in the kitchen when they were washing dishes. "Remember how it's been for him, trying to get better. You must let him alone." He didn't want to hunt anymore, she meant. On his precious Saturdays and Sundays he wanted only to lie and read, or sometimes to go to the park, and her mother wanted to be with him on those two days out of the whole week. He came first. "Chris?" she would say. "Chris—?" coming into a room where there was only Nina, as if she wanted always to know where he was, *how* he was. These two had their own private world. But that was all right. Nina had hers. She knew that for them to hunt for another place was only to become more depressed, to conclude that perhaps this apartment "for the money," her mother would say, wasn't so bad after all. "We must save," she would say. "That's the important thing now. If we can manage to save, we'll do better later."

"The most I seem to do is the best I can for today," her father had answered, which for him took out the struggle. It was her little, energetic, pent-up, strung-up mother who struggled and planned and looked to the future. But not, thought Nina, to getting out of here.

"Well, I'll tell you what," she said suddenly, turning and hooking an arm around her father's neck and feeling, against her will, an odd, down-turning sort of smile twist the corners of her mouth as if it couldn't help itself because she loved him, "if you two won't hunt—I *will*. I swear I'll find something myself."

She curled herself into a ball under her tucked-in blankets on the couch. The rain was still falling, but quietly. The wind had dropped. In the darkness it all came back: the boy and what they had said to each other at the top of the park, and how he had told her about the French Museum. Again she saw Lisabetta racing like a mad thing across the grass, and "Oh, Lisabetta, you silly cat," then, "Oh-goost!" called Mam'-zelle, "Oh-goost!" And she remembered the feeling she'd had running up the walk toward the museum doors: "I'm coming! I'm coming!" But to whom had she called, to whom made this promise? To someone, or to the museum itself? "I knew you'd come," said the girl, folded up in the depths of shadow, her hand flickering over Lisabetta's head. "There's time for you and me —plenty of time. But come back. Of course you'll come back." *Yet why "of course"?* How had the girl known to say "of course"? Because I *will* go back, Nina told herself. I will always go back. That is my place. And tomorrow will be Saturday.

In the night she dreamed she was alone in some unknown town, putting coins into a telephone box, desperately, because she was late and far from home, but could not remember her own number, and the print was so small and the light so dim that she could not find it in the book. "If you are new," the cool voice said, "you will not be in the book." And nobody could tell her the number, though she was given person after person, remote, uncaring, until all her money was gone. "But my mother will be frantic—time is passing—" "Time is a river without banks," said the cool voice. "If there are no banks, there is nothing for time to pass."

Chapter Four

Nina, with Mrs. Staynes's umbrella, arrived at a quarter past ten at the museum the next morning, and saw with a sense of outraged, violated possession, two big yellow school buses outside the gates, which meant that the whole building would be seething. She'd return the umbrella and until all those kids were gone, she would visit that ferny, wooded place she had seen across the lawn from the small dining room.

The shoving mass of bodies was gathered in the central hall, one group now being led off toward the south wing, another upstairs, and Mrs. Staynes apparently was just beginning to give directions to a third about the north wing where the rooms were. *My* wing. Nina stared at her resentfully, but caught her eye over the heads of the children and held up the umbrella and nodded, and Mrs. Staynes motioned her to leave it at the desk. Then she waved a hand as if to say, "Why not come along?" The last thing Nina wanted was to go along, though after all, if she felt like it she could escape.

Mrs. Staynes held up her hands for quiet and Nina

studied her minutely, as if memorizing her: the rather round mouth with its clear-cut lips, the short, definite nose, deep-set eyes, high forehead and thick brown hair, coiled up and pierced, as yesterday, by two "sticks," Nina called them, but today they were different, not metal, she thought, but maybe ivory. She highly approved of the way Mrs. Staynes looked—fresh and tailored, but easy in her clothes. I won't look like that for years, and Mother still doesn't. I wonder why not—is it because we haven't much money?

"Now I want you to be quiet again," Mrs. Staynes said. "*Everybody*." They all hushed. "I've told you about the rooms we have here, and that we're going to play a game. You'll have to be watchful and use your eyes every instant. You can't go laughing and talking and joking and pushing if you want to have any success. Somewhere in these rooms is an amethyst ring, a ring with a clear lavender stone like glass, only of course it isn't glass but a gem. This is the one I mean." She held up a large painted drawing of a ring, showing quite distinctly the cut of the stone and the color of it. "It will be in plain view where you can't miss it if you really look. I'm not saying it's an actual ring you could put on. It might, for instance, be part of a scene in one of the big tapestries. Does everyone understand? Remember not to touch anything and that you have an hour." She smiled. "Oh, yes—there are prizes."

Nina followed as they all moved off, but the magic, the inexpressible specialness of the place was gone. She hung behind; this was not her school—she knew no one. She would have liked to ask Mrs. Staynes who the girl in the little bedroom could have been but Mrs. Staynes had already disappeared behind a door marked STAFF, leaving someone named Miss Landsdowne in charge.

When the main part of the crowd had pushed as far as the first room, which was the library, and had spilled into it, Nina went on ahead filled with assurance that the girl would be waiting for her. But when she stepped through the doorway of the little bedroom she saw in an instant that no one was there. It was filled with sun streaming in through the trees; its walls reflected a green light as though it were a shell lying on the bottom of the sea, and it seemed, because of the moving branches outside, itself to be moving. The floor shone like honey or brook water; it had a deep look. She went toward the closet bed trying to pierce the shadows behind the half-drawn curtains as though an intensity of looking might bring the girl into being, curled there with Lisabetta crouched, dozing and purring at her side. But no form emerged, though Nina stood at the bedside as if expecting some act of magic.

She went into the hall, following it round through the entire wing from one room to another, glancing into each and knowing by some odd second sense that the one she wanted was not there even before her eyes had finished searching.

The girl was in the music room on the opposite side of the wing. It was a corner room at the back, whose windows commanded a view over a sea of lawn stretching toward the gardens at the far end of the grounds. She was standing behind a harp two heads taller than herself, her arms extended on either side of it, running her fingers over the strings, though she was only pretending to play; there was no sound.

"Not very satisfactory," she said, and turned to the harpsichord, sat down at the chair in front of it, and ran her hands over the keys as though she had played all her life. But the keys were not depressed. "Of course I hear in my mind what I'm playing. You wouldn't guess, would you, that I could play both instruments so well that Papa often called me in to give concerts for his dignitaries. In a way, it's humiliating. *Farfelou!*" She gave a resigned shrug, then looked up at Nina, smiling a derisive smile. "Those dolts of children! Only one boy will find the ring, and one girl, out of the whole lot of them. You wouldn't believe it! They don't really see. People don't. You could put a thing in front of their noses."

Nina studied the vivid, changing face and felt in the girl a quickness, a kind of light, flickering nervousness, quite different from yesterday, as if she were in an entirely different mood. "If I were looking for the ring," Nina said shyly, "I'd probably be a dolt, too—probably stare straight at it—" She blinked. For on the fourth finger of the girl's right hand, which at this moment hovered over the lid of the harpsicord, was the amethyst ring. She remembered afterwards that it had seemed neither too large nor too pretentious for the hand that rested for a second or two on the instrument. It looked right, as if it had been created for that hand as an expression of the personality of the girl who now seemed older in some indefinable way than Nina, though they were of about the same height and Nina had taken it for granted they were near the same age. Yet suddenly she was not sure—not at all sure. For she could take in now, in the clear light of morning, the finely boned face, velvety skin, the large, lustrous eyes and tawny hair hanging in curves to the girl's shoulders. Nina felt rough by contrast, awkwardly aware of herself in a way she had never been before. The girl had a long dress but there was none of the clumsiness and homeliness about it of those long dresses the girls were wearing to school. It was of some thin silky material that Nina wanted to touch. She had no idea what it was, nor could she make up her mind about the color: seeming now smoky, a kind of blue-gray, then sea-color, elusive and changing.

"Is *that* the ring Mrs. Staynes—?"

"In a manner of speaking, yes." But there was a glint of amusement in the girl's eye and one eyebrow went up. She might have been any age, yet why Nina felt this she couldn't have told. "Listen, they're coming. I want to talk to you, but not here, not with this mob around. Meet me in the courtyard in half an hour. The guards won't bother you there and we can do as we please. They'll suspect you of being mental if you go around talking to yourself the way you were doing yesterday." She gave a little laugh, got up and went to the door, and directly she had gone five or six boys pushed in, rushed from painting to painting shouting at each other, then hung over a case on whose shelves ancient instruments were laid out. But these had nothing to do with the search and they rushed out again.

Nina went to the window, her face burning. So it was the girl she had felt standing in the doorway behind her when she had ordered the maid to put flowers on the table and Auguste to bring wood for the fire. What a fool she must have looked—*and* sounded! I swear I will never talk to myself again—I swear it. Yes, but what a comfortable habit it is. And when a person's been doing it for a long time, walking home through the woods after school or getting up early to run out along the creek bank, it's a habit not easily broken.

"Come on, now—better get along, kid. Stay with your school." It was one of the guards, a plump, bored-looking old man with a red face and bilious eyes, standing there looking at her, his hands behind his back in the immemorial position of guards. Perhaps because he had hairs in his nose and tufts sticking out of his ears, Nina took an instant dislike to him. She hated being called "kid."

In ten minutes, having discovered the courtyard, which was quite deserted, and seeing it all secluded with stone benches in clumps of greenery and a fountain splashing and stone children standing here and there, half hidden, she hovered on the verge with a sense of indescribable expectancy, but would not let herself put even a foot into it until the appointed time. Long glass doors opened onto its flagstones and the smell of it was damp earth and bark and roots and ferns, and the fragrance of flowers that grew in sheltered places.

She went back to the central hall where everyone in Mrs. Staynes's group was gathered. Suddenly at ease, no longer wanting to stand at the back, she jostled her way forward and stood there, listening to conversations and wondering idly what the prizes might be. She'd heard Miss Landsdowne say you could choose.

"I want everyone who has seen the ring to come here to me," said Mrs. Staynes. Several pushed to the front and stood near her, and when Nina hesitated, uncertain as to whether she should, Mrs. Staynes held out a hand.

"Yes, Nina, why not? It makes no difference about the school. Now each of you, one at a time, will tell me where you saw the ring."

Each did, and then stood back waiting, and when Nina went to her and whispered that she had seen the ring on the hand of a girl in the music room, Mrs. Staynes, who had been leaning over so as to present an intimate ear, raised up and gazed at her. "But not a ring on a real person, Nina," she said. "No, it wouldn't be *this* ring—this one is in the possession of the museum."

"A ring on a real person!" jeered a boy in the front. "Rabbithead!"

Nina, humiliated, went and stood next to him so that she could give him a good jab with her elbow, which he returned with vigor, and she stood there furious because she had been too sure of herself. As the girl had foretold, two had seen the ring in the only place it could be seen: in a portrait, hanging in one of the large bedrooms, of a young woman, *Dominique, Reading* by Jean Louis Baptiste Chrysostome.

Nina went off at once and found the portrait in an inconspicuous position between two chests. The young woman's head, from which hung a thin veil, was inclined just slightly above the pages of her book, her ivory flesh lambent against a dark background in the light of a candle flame, her lips curved in an ironic smile as if she were dryly amused at what she was reading. One hand supported her chin; the other rested in the shadow of the veil that hung in folds to the table. Within that shadow the amethyst stone of the ring and its gold setting caught a gleam from the flame. Yes, it *was* "in plain view where you couldn't miss it if you really looked." But the trick was in the looking; to the quick, careless glance, the ring was scarcely there.

"So that's it," Nina said to the painting. "The ring has come down to the girl, handed on generation after generation. This is probably her great-grandmother when *she* was young." The resemblance was astonishing.

Chapter Five

Stepping through the doorway of the library into the courtyard and at first seeing no one, Nina went from stone child to stone child to look into their faces, each quite individual, brushed with moving splotches of sunlight, the lips lightly, inscrutably smiling, and the eyes, though blank, gazing back with an expression of serene gaiety. Nina wanted to reach out and touch a cheek, stroke an arm or a leg, the stone looked so inviting, not gray but a warm sun color.

"When I was a child," said the girl's voice behind her as though taking up a conversation interrupted only a moment before, and Nina turned, and there she was, sitting on a bench with one leg crossed over the other and her hands clasped round her knee, "when I was a child I wanted them to come alive, and I would talk to them. They were in the courtyard of my home in France, near Saint-Sauveur in the province of Burgundy, standing about, just as they do here. I loved them as my friends. They have names, you know—the boy over there on the other side of the fountain is Cyprian, and the two next to him, Stephane and Chiro, and the girls are Odile and Simone and Gabrielle." She pointed to each in turn. "Their names suit them, don't you think? I used to talk to them as if they were alive, but then I've always been much alone. Perhaps I'm a little odd. Are you?" she asked, as though inquiring after Nina's health.

Nina went to the girl and sat beside her, and she noticed that now they were hidden in this semicircle of flowering tulip trees and could not be seen from the open doors of the library. She looked at the girl with seriousness. "I don't know. Do you mean because I talk to myself? Perhaps I *am* odd. I've never thought about it. But I like being alone, or with my cat. I've never minded. Tell me your name. I can't go on thinking about you with no name to call you by. Mine's Nina."

"Yes, I know. Mine is Dominique, though I've usually been called Domi except by my grandmother, who was a very formal old lady. She never liked things by halves, never any undue familiarity. And when I must cry, I am to go away by myself in private, and often, by the time I reach my room, there is nothing left, no tears, only a small, hard lump inside my chest." Dominique again, as she had in the music room, lifted an eyebrow and gave a quick, mirthless laugh. "Even when my father is shot, I hide myself so as not to offend her by my abandonment to grief, though she herself is as desolate as I. But she would spare neither of us so much as a drop of mercy. What is—*is*. Yes, of course, I have always known that. I remember the way she stands in front of me, very upright, and her voice is like a crackle of paper being crushed. 'Your father has been shot,' she says. That is all. Then she turns away—to hide her face, I know now. And I often think how a moment of touching is the difference between complete, hopeless despair and being able to endure. I mean, if we can put our arms around one another. But Grandmother and I rarely touched—perhaps her lips might brush my cheek if I was leaving to be gone for some time, but that was all." Dominique stopped, then her voice deepened with tenderness. "My father was *very* different."

Nina stared at her. Her father had been shot. And she thought of her own father, how he had come to her last night and put his arms around her. "Squirrel," he called her. She couldn't remember when he had begun it—she had always been called that, but only by him, a private, special name that never seemed to come to her mother's lips. And there had been a special feeling between them as long as she could recall, not spoken of but wordlessly present, so that she could not bear the thought in this instant of how fiercely she had resented his illness that had forced them to leave the mountains— even resented *him.* She wanted to find him and tell him: thank God he was not shot; he was alive and she loved him.

Struck suddenly by a curious quality in the silence, Nina came to herself, and it seemed to her that Dominique had withdrawn, as if she had actually paled, thinned, somehow lost substance.

"I thought that that painting," Nina began loudly, as if to bring Dominique back from some great distance and feeling a strange, quicksilver dart of fear go feathering down the backs of her arms. Yet now, hearing her own voice braying in the stillness of the courtyard, she again felt herself clumsy and awkward in contrast to this pale, elegant being with the tawny hair and long dress and black slippers. Great scuffed boats her own shoes looked beside them, so she tucked hers back under the bench. Also, she was conscious of her hands and her nails, which she'd never particularly thought about before. "I wondered," she said in a more ordinary voice, "if that might be your grandmother—or great-grandmother in the painting. You know, the one with the ring."

Dominique slid her a little sideways glance of exactly the shade of ironic amusement that curled the young woman's lips in the painting as she read. "She is myself, Dominique de Lombre, Comtesse de Bernonville. A good likeness. Chrysostome painted me several times. He was a very dear friend of my father's though I saw him rarely—only when he came to the château to paint the family."

"But the painting!" cried Nina. "Surely it's not—not *new*."

Dominique burst out laughing and her eyes almost closed in merriment. "Modern, you mean. You don't understand, do you? Of course not. How could you possibly? But I shall explain. First of all—"

"First of all," Nina interrupted, annoyed at being laughed at, "what did you mean yesterday—you *knew* I would come? How did you? I just might not have, not ever."

Dominique studied her for a moment with an unreadable look out of eyes of so deep a purple as to appear at times almost black.

"No, no." She wagged a first finger back and forth. "Not possible. You had to come. But you are quite right—an explanation is the first business at hand, because otherwise I should have to make you wait too long before that question would be answered. Well, to begin with, after my father had gone and I was living in these rooms alone in the château with my grandmother—except for the servants, of course—"

"*These* rooms!" exclaimed Nina.

"*Zut alors!*" Dominique shrugged with impatience and threw up her hands. "Haven't you read the little signs tacked in the entranceways? I should say that first of all you must learn thoroughness. These rooms are from my home in France, the furnishings, the doors, the carved panelings, the chandeliers—all brought here for the museum, even my stone children and these benches and the fountain and the flagstones and that sundial up there on the wall, set in place here in this strange city in another land, just as they were at home.

"But it is *not* the same! I loved every brick and stone of my home, and the views out across the woods and fields from every window. If I were away, I couldn't wait to get back. So that this is a kind of strange, twisted dream of my home, the same and yet weirdly not the same. But it was simply not possible for me to stay there in Saint-Sauveur, watching those barbarians tear my château to pieces in order to modernize, as they put it. I loathed them.

"But about you. One night after my father is imprisoned and shot, I have a dream. And you must remember that this is long, *long* before my home is torn apart and the pieces brought here. In my dream my father is trying to tell me something, and I am trying desperately to understand, so desperately that I must be

[43]

sobbing in my sleep because when I wake up my throat is burning. In the dream I know all at once that I am no longer at the château but in some other building that is full of echoing halls with rooms opening off of them that I recognize are like the rooms of my home and yet are terribly unlike. Here are pieces of our furniture, some of the tables, chairs, cabinets, beds, scattered about, but all placed so strangely, with no beloved bibelots—no small personal possessions, none of our *little* things. It all looks so unlived with, so cold. And there are strange people wandering about, people in cut-off ugly clothing, and I am enraged by the air they have of the *right* to be wandering about. 'Go away!' I cry at them. 'Go away! This is private property—' but they pay no attention to me. And when I stand at one of the big windows to look out on my own countryside, I think I am going mad. For what do I see? Not the orchards and fields and woods and red-tiled roofs of my village, but tall buildings and strange carriages that speed along terrifyingly by themselves, with no horses, no way of being drawn. And they move quite silently, though occasionally piercing squeaks are heard or other loud noises that seem to be warnings. 'Aa-aarnk, aaa-rrnk!' they cry every so often—"

"Honking," murmured Nina, keeping her voice low so as not really to interrupt.

"*Hong*-king, you say?" returned Dominique, and the word sounded so incongruous on her lips as almost to lose meaning. "Hong-king! A preposterous word, one I still do not know, but this is possibly because of my situation. I see these dreadful carriages out there across the lawn, beyond the stone walls, and there are no cot-

[44]

tages but apparently some great city and I am in the midst of it.

"I turn away from the window and run crying through this strange building. Oh, the desolate, lonely sorrow of one's dreams. And there is no answer—no comfort—"

"I know—I know," whispered Nina, her eyes fixed with intensity on Domi's face, and recalling the grief of that dream she had had only last night in which she had been trying hopelessly to telephone her mother from some nameless town.

"And presently," Dominique went on, "presently I come to our small dining room and because Mama and Papa and I have always eaten there when we're alone so that I feel it to be especially private, I stop at the door and look in. And there is a girl walking toward the windows and ordering the maid to put yellow tulips on the table and then Auguste to bring wood for the fire. Oh, I like that girl! She reminds me of myself, talking to no one, making up scenes, pretending. And I feel very warm toward her, comforted somehow, because we might understand one another. And yet because I know that the right moment has not arrived for us to meet, I turn away.

"And now I come to my little bedroom—mine, and yet no longer mine, and there is Lisabetta, my cat, my own cat. 'Lisabetta!' I call to her, and she comes to me at once and when I go to the bed and crawl onto it and try to hide myself at the back of it in my bewildered misery, she hops up and comes and sits by me and purrs her song of contentment and love and companionship.

"Then, in my dream, I see you standing at the doorway and in the darkened air the lightning flashes and we stare at one another—and I see my father standing behind you. I see him, though he is already dead. There is some connection between you, between the two of you. And then you turn and run away—you run right through him—but my father stands looking at me and he smiles and nods with the greatest assurance as if to say, 'She will help us, Domi. She is the one who will help us.' There is no doubt in my mind as to what he means. And then he vanishes from my sight, and I wake up with my throat on fire, and every smallest detail of that dream burned into my mind forever."

Domi was still sitting upright with one leg crossed over the other and her hands clasped round her knee, and she was looking away across the courtyard with her eyes wide, staring at nothing tangible as though still lost in that bewildering dream. Nina, rather hunched, clutching herself in her folded arms, was turned sideways with her gaze fixed on Domi's face. She waited, but the girl did not continue.

"And then, Domi—? Was that all?"

"Yes," said Dominique, "that was all. *All.* Never do I see my father in my dreams again, but as time goes on, I understand more and more deeply that I can do nothing for him alone and that I must speak to you in this moment when you finally come to the museum and we meet at last."

"What did you feel when you saw me yesterday? Were you astonished that your dream had turned out?"

"Not really. But I say to myself, 'How can this young creature help me—my father and me? It seems

utterly unlikely, utterly unimaginable. You seem so—"
Dominique shrugged, and her eyebrows went up, "how
shall I say? So uncomplex for this work. I don't mean
unintelligent, but not learned enough, not experienced
enough. Yes, that is the word. Now Mrs. Staynes—if
she had appeared in my dream, engaged as she is in writing a life of my father, then I would understand. Ah, but
even so," and again Dominique's first finger wagged
back and forth, "fate chooses perhaps wisely. I have
no way of talking to Mrs. Staynes. It would be quite
impossible—but to you, my fresh, eager, open-minded
young friend, I can say anything. Yes, I feel that. Oh,
but I *must* feel it! And so now—I ask you. Will you help
us, Nina? My father and me? Have you the stomach
for it, as they say in your country?"

Nina swallowed. "But I don't understand. What
do you mean, the stomach for it? How does my stomach
come in?" She asked this in such baffled amazement that
Dominique burst into another peal of laughter.

"Oh, my!" She laughed until the tears came to her
eyes. "You don't know this expression? Well, good for
me. How much I have picked up! It means, *ma chérie*,
it means—have you the inner fortitude, the strength?"

Nina was silent for a little, trying to take this in,
trying to work her way toward some understanding
of all Dominique had been saying, and she was about
to speak when Dominique suddenly gave a cry of
exasperated despair.

"There *must* be some mistake. *Why* would I be given
you? You look—really, child, sitting there with your
mouth open, you look at this moment, if you will forgive me, as if you haven't a brain in your head."

Nina straightened and drew in her breath. "I don't know what it is I'm supposed to do. But I do know one thing—I have a brain in my head. I didn't mean I wondered what having a stomach for anything meant. I meant I wondered why I would need a strong stomach. But it isn't only that—in fact, that's the least of it. About the ring and who would find it, you knew ahead. So that I don't see why you need me at all."

Domi studied her for a moment as if turning over her full meaning. Then all at once she smiled. "I have these odd, quick intuitions, Nina. I have small knowledges, but believe me, I'm not prescient. What you and I can perhaps do together is something quite different. It is nothing small, quick, easy, nothing here and now that I can get hold of. I can't see into it. About you I have just now changed my mind. Will you forgive me?" She held out her hand, palm down, so that the amethyst flashed, and Nina was about to grasp that hand when Domi suddenly withdrew it. "No," she said. "No, I can't—not yet. I can't test you that far. There are other matters that must be got through first." Then she looked away. "If Mrs. Staynes should ask you any questions, let her know whatever you must, what you are able. We'll see each other again, and when we do, I'll of course tell you all you need to know about my father and me. I think, Nina, don't you, that we're going to be friends—fast friends?"

Again Dominique's face took on its expression of appealing openness and Nina felt herself respond to it with an irresistible rush of warmth. Yes, they would be friends—why shouldn't they? And she felt this all the more deeply and strongly because of the peculiar privacy of each of their meetings, nothing secret on purpose, but seeming to come about in this way. And then, Nina had never known anyone even remotely like Dominique.

Dominique got up and moved off, and Nina was about to say something when she heard footsteps. She got up to see who it was and, having seen, turned back again. But Dominique was gone.

Chapter Six

"Nina!" said Helena Staynes. "You're still here! Good —I must talk to you. Are you expected home for lunch? Well, look, if you'd like to come down to Auguste's cottage and have a bite with us, why not phone home and ask if you can stay? And use the phone on Mr. Quarles's desk to call—it'll be on the museum considering that I was the rabbithead, not you. Do you know where the cottage is? Over under the trees on the south side of the grounds—the side nearest the park. We'll expect you, then—shall we?"

Mrs. Staynes continued through the courtyard and out the gate at the back, and Nina, filled with delight and a baffled curiosity, ran into the library, along the corridor and through to old Mr. Quarles's desk. Why was Mrs. Staynes a rabbithead?

Ten minutes later she stood in the entranceway of Auguste's cottage, the door of which had been left open to the sun and the fresh, rich, grass-smelling air; Auguste and Philippe had been mowing the lawns sitting astride the big mowing machines. She hesitated there, taking it all in, details which she made out bit by bit for, compared to the brilliance of the day, the interior was dim: the whitewashed walls, red-tiled floor, the enormous dark fireplace with a single beam across the top, potted plants on the windowsills and, along one of them, Lisabetta stretched asleep in the sun. Nina had a general impression of newspapers dropped on the floor near one of the chairs and a jacket and shoes left lying about, but why not? Auguste lived here alone. At a long refectory table set with a carton of milk, a pot of jam, a partially cut loaf, a cheese, two or three bowls and a teapot, the boy of the park and Mrs. Staynes were eating their lunch. At the far end Auguste was rolling and slapping and kneading a mass of dough, and Nina could smell the nutty, buttery fragrance of it. It was home, that smell. The home up at Silverspring.

"Nice, isn't it?" said the boy. "Auguste's cottage, I mean. Remember I told you he came with Mam'zelle from France? She promised him a cottage just like the one he had over there, and this is it." He was looking at her as if he knew exactly how surprised she was at seeing him here—surprised at everything!—and was tickled by it. He was watching her, and he was grinning. "Ever know a gardener who made his own bread?"

Mrs. Staynes held out a hand for Nina to come and sit down, and Nina went over. "My mother used to bake bread," she said, "but she hasn't time now."

"You like bought bread?" demanded Auguste, rolling and thumping the bread dough.

"I can't stand it. It hasn't any taste at all—"

"Just what we think," said Mrs. Staynes, "so thank

the Lord for Auguste. Here, Nina, try this piece buttered, with some of that sharp cheese on it. And have some of the sliced tomatoes and cucumbers. That's Auguste's French dressing on them—he's a champion salad maker."

Nina stood there looking at Lisabetta asleep in the sun, at the sun-dappled walls of Auguste's cottage and the comfortable chairs here and there, and at Auguste and the boy and Mrs. Staynes. She couldn't get over it: that she had been invited here to be with them, already, and she scarcely knew them. The boy and Mrs. Staynes must have sensed her thought because they both laughed suddenly, as if with her over her pleasure, while Auguste pressed the dough flat, cut it in half, made two loaf-sized rolls, put them in pans and buttered their tops, then went into the kitchen where he must have put them somewhere to rise.

"Gil told me your name," said Mrs. Staynes. "Did you wonder, Nina? He said he heard the others call you that, yesterday up in the park."

"Oh," said Nina. "Gil. And now I know your name," she said, sitting down beside Mrs. Staynes. "Helena Hampton Staynes. I saw it on Mr. Quarles's desk, and it reminds me of England. Can you guess why?" She looked from Gil to Mrs. Staynes. "It's a game Dad and I play." But they couldn't guess, though you could see by the look on Gil's face that he thought he ought to be able to, that he was the kind of person who ought. "Stained glass windows and Hampton Court," said Nina. "I've never been to Hampton Court, but Dad has, when he was a boy, being taken around the British Isles by his parents." She buttered the thick slice of Auguste's bread, then cut lots of cheese and put the slices neatly over and helped herself to salad.

There was a little silence during which Auguste drank off the rest of his tea, then went outside to finish the mowing. Nina, filled with peaceful joy, ate her sandwich with her elbows on the table and stared around at every last thing in the cottage, which satisfied her to the core of her being. It was untidy, her mother would have said, with Auguste's belongings tossed around, but she liked it that way. And she liked it that neither Gil nor Mrs. Staynes seemed to feel under any compulsion to keep up a conversation, as though she were company. In this little space of quietness they continued to eat, Auguste started up his mower and moved off, the wind could be heard blowing in the tops of the trees, Lisabetta stretched herself on the windowsill and yawned hugely, then settled again, her nose in the root of her tail. And Gil turned his fiery blue eyes on Nina and she noted for the first time that they were not just blue, but had a greenish light in them. Serenely she met his gaze, thinking how she had never seen eyes of just that color before.

"Nina," said Mrs. Staynes finally, "I want to apologize to you for being clumsy in front of everyone. When you whispered to me that you'd seen the ring on the finger of a girl in the music room, instead of whispering back, I said out loud that of course it wouldn't be on a real person, which put you in an embarrassing position."

"You mean it made me look stupid? Well, I was."

"Oh, no," said Mrs. Staynes. "No, I don't think you were being stupid in the least, and neither does

Gil. I think that having looked at that drawing I held up, you were certain you'd seen the ring I meant, and you were certain you'd won. Was it on the hand of someone you thought might be on the staff?"

Nina's eyes slid away from the eyes watching her —Gil's and Mrs. Staynes's—steady and asking. So, then, they had been talking about her, the two of them. They had decided she'd had a reason. Her heart quickened.

"I made a mistake," she answered lightly. "There're probably dozens of amethyst rings. I saw in the bedroom the painting of the woman reading, and I had a good look at it, at the ring. No wonder only two saw it. That was very clever to choose the ring to be found. It seems to come out of the painting at you the longer you stare at it, so that instead of *any* ring, it's the one in the drawing you showed us and no mistake. It's a kind of magic, isn't it—what the painter did."

She had her self-possession again, and knew it. But even as she sat there, relaxed, eating her bread and cheese, a conversation with herself was flashing back and forth in her mind. I'm keeping Domi secret. Why am I? I feel I want to, that I have to, but why? Domi said to tell Mrs. Staynes whatever I must, or am able to. What a strange thing to say, and what did she mean? But it's exactly what I'm doing because I can't seem to help it. She looked up again, and Mrs. Staynes had apparently been waiting for her to come to.

"I chose the ring," Mrs. Staynes said, "not only because of the magic of that painting, but because I'm very much attached to it. You see, I own it. It's a treasure of mine."

Nina's face went blank. "You *own* it!"

"Yes. Long before I started the biography I'm working on, I'd been fascinated by the de Lombre family—the family that once owned the furniture and everything we have of these rooms here in the museum. When I was in France some years ago, I heard they were going to tear the château apart, so I told Mrs. Henry about it. And when I was in Paris in a little antique shop, I was struck by the likeness of a ring they had in the jewelry case to the one in the painting, and when I examined the ring, I found the family crest inside the setting, up near the stone. Of course I bought it—but for me, not for the museum."

"But how *can* it be the same ring?" demanded Nina in utter bewilderment. "Your ring—and Dominique's?"

"And why not, Nina? Why not? It is. We've taken the magnifying glass to the painting and compared the two. What with the family crest, there can be no mistake. I wish I could wear it, but it's a little too large for my fourth finger, which is where it belongs, and I wouldn't let a jeweler touch it. I must someday, but I seem to have a superstition about it. Do you like our rooms? Do they mean to you what you thought they would?"

"Oh, yes," Nina said in a tranced voice, scarcely hearing herself speak. How could both Domi and Mrs. Staynes have the ring? They couldn't; Mrs. Staynes only thinks she has. No, but I don't believe that, unless there are two, and I don't believe that either. Again, as it had once before—just when, she couldn't remember —the feathery chill rippled round the back of her neck and down her arms. "I had the Feeling," she said, still hardly aware of what she was saying, "my Museum Feeling in the little dining room—"

"Your museum feeling—what is that?"

Nina was leaning on one arm, studying the grain of the wood in the table, a golden grain lying beneath layers of wax. The wood was silken with polishing, Nina found, when she slipped the side of her hand over it. What was Mrs. Staynes saying? Oh, yes—

"I can't explain exactly. I've never had it so strong before—never just like that—in any other museum, not in the one up in Silverspring, nor in the museum over in Golden Gate Park. I love museums and what's in them—things that are very old. Did Gil tell you I want to be a curator?"

Nina saw Gil and Mrs. Staynes send each other a glance: was he perhaps supposed not to have told? He'd been listening and watching her. She had a feeling he had been shaping an idea of her, quietly, all to himself, and she would never know what that idea was.

"But of course you don't become a curator right off," Mrs. Staynes said. "It's not easy, especially for women. To become head, that is. The director of a museum."

"I don't expect so. But it doesn't matter. Is that what you are?"

"No, Nina, I'm the registrar, the one who oversees the cataloging of every object that comes in—I see that they are all kept track of. Mrs. Henry—the one they call Mam'zelle—is the chief curator, the director. There are different kinds of curators, you know. This is her museum; she owns it."

"Yes, Gil told me."

They had each had a slice of the chocolate cake Helena Staynes had brought in a cardboard box. Now Mrs. Staynes finished hers then pushed back her chair and stretched herself with her arms folded behind her head.

"Oh," she said, "I don't want to go. I never do. I feel such peace here in Auguste's cottage that I want to stay forever. But I must be off—I must!"

"Me, too," said Gil. "Gotta go," just as he had said it in the park, Nina remembered. He had his private affairs to attend to. What would they be?

She went, now, to Lisabetta and leaned over and buried her face in the cat's warm, breathing side, in the glossy fur that smelled of new-cut grass, and Lisabetta lifted her head and inquired "Mung-goww?" out of her sleep and yawned in Nina's face, then studied her very seriously and directly out of eyes the blue of hyacinths. Nina raised up and stared out of the window while she absently stroked Lisabetta, who turned on her side and began to purr. "My Lisabetta—my little queen," Auguste had called her yesterday. Yet Domi had said, "Lisabetta, my cat—" or "my own cat—"; something like that. And what possible connection could there be between Dominique, with her filmy dress and black slippers—and Auguste?

"Mrs. Staynes, does Auguste have a daughter?"

"No—no daughter, Nina. No family at all."

Lisabetta, then, was like the ring that could not belong to two people. And yet did.

Chapter Seven

Nina saw Gil occasionally at school and he would nod, with a quick lift of an eyebrow, and raise an arm just briefly. But she did not see Dominique again for some time. It rained steadily over Sunday and continued to rain for several days, and Nina was expected to come straight home from school.

"But *why*, Mother—what on earth difference does rain make? Anyone would think I was tubercular!"

"I would simply feel better," Mrs. Harmsworth said, "after that other awful time and I don't want you getting soaked running all over the neighborhood and staying out until past dinner. Why must you keep harping about that museum, Nina?"

Nina stared in astonishment at the injustice of the question. Why, she'd hardly mentioned it. She hadn't harped; she couldn't remember harping once. But all *right*. She would keep this in mind. And on Friday morning, a gray, quiet morning, she promised herself privately that now she would search out Dominique again, for Domi, too, must have been eager for another meeting, filled with a sharp impatience.

"Daddy has to work late," Mrs. Harmsworth said at breakfast, "so I thought I'd wait for him and then we'd eat downtown and go to a show afterwards. We haven't done that for months—"

"By yourselves, you mean," and Nina saw an odd, guilty look come into her mother's face. "But why shouldn't you? It's not raining and I could—" She caught herself on the brink of the four forbidden words.

"It's a picture we've been waiting for—I don't think you'd like it, Nina." Which meant, Nina knew, that her mother thought it too old for her.

"But I said I didn't care. Will you leave me anything to eat or shall I fix an egg and some toast?"

That afternoon, after school, Nina knew instantly, the moment she entered the museum, that something was wrong. Perhaps her feeling had to do with the fact that she had seen Mrs. Staynes and Auguste outside, Mrs. Staynes in a vivid purple suit making agitated gestures: pointing to the paths on the far side of the lawns and then waving her hand over the flower beds at her feet. Inside the museum it was nothing at first that anybody said or did; only there was something Nina sensed. Mr. Quarles was speaking in low, disapproving tones to another much younger man at the information desk, and then suddenly a little woman in cherry red— the little woman of the upstairs window who had called out "Oh, Lisabetta, you silly cat!" and directed Auguste to do various things about the gardens—came out of the door marked VICTORINE HENRY, DIRECTOR and hurried over to them.

"Has it been found yet?" she asked. "Have they found it?" Mr. Quarles shook his head and the little dark woman said "Tchk!" and crossed the rotunda to the big doors and stepped outside. The men went on talking and Nina stood in front of the painting *Time Is a River Without Banks* without actually seeing it, but using her nerve endings keenly, as a dog uses its sense of smell, snuffing the air for delicate intimations. Several of the museum guards came and went past Mr. Quarles and the young man, each in turn saying, "No, nothing," or "No luck."

Presently Mrs. Staynes came in with Auguste and the little dark woman, whom Mrs. Staynes called Victorine, and Mrs. Staynes was explaining something to Auguste, who was looking as if yes, he'd understood all this the first time, but there wasn't anything he could do but go on doing what he *had* been.

He went out, and after a little Mrs. Staynes and Mrs. Henry turned away and disappeared into Mrs. Henry's office. As she passed, Nina smiled at Mrs. Staynes, but her expression, though her eyes flicked over Nina's face, did not change from one of distraught unhappiness into recognition. And when the younger man had gone upstairs, Nina went over to Mr. Quarles's desk to find out what the trouble was, but first the telephone rang and then a group of people came to the desk to ask questions. And, finally, when Mr. Quarles became absorbed in a long conversation with the last of them, Nina turned away discouraged.

Everything was wrong.

The old red-faced whiskery guard, with the sprouts of hair in his nose and ears, caught sight of Nina going into the little courtyard and followed her there and looked at her. Well, what did *he* want? What was *he* suspicious of? The soft gray day had turned clear and bright as the afternoon deepened, and through the archway with its iron gate that opened into the outer grounds, the sun flooded into the courtyard, its beams broken by the leaves of the tulip trees on whose shining surfaces it made flickering glints. The plumes of water in the fountain sparkled. The stone children stood in glancing sun and shadow, and the changing light seemed to give them perpetually changing expressions. When, momentarily, first one and then another stood wholly in shadow, the stone became luminous under their chins, their noses, under the caves of their eye sockets, and on the palms of their outheld hands. It was a luminosity cast up from the sunny flagstones, and it made the children seem magical, as though, at any moment, they might be about to speak.

But the perfection of the afternoon and the stone children and the courtyard, which smelled intoxicatingly of rain-soaked earth and mosses and plants, was of course spoiled by the presence of Old Whiskers. Nina sat on Dominique's bench, pushed away a little book that had been left lying there, put her own books down and opened her binder, then looked up. Well, her cold eyes asked him, what's wrong? Is there any harm in my sitting here and doing my homework undisturbed? Whiskers walked on, as if he read her eyes, made a tour of the courtyard, and went in at the library doors. She was now out of his sight.

"Dominique!" she called softly, her head bent over her binder. "I'm here—I'm ready." She waited, pretending to work. But nothing happened. Nina glanced up and around. There was no Dominique. And Nina sensed, as she had sensed the undercurrent of tension in the museum, that Dominique would not come. Was she angry? Had Nina stayed away too long? She got up and explored the courtyard, going hot and cold for some glimpse of that teasing, ageless face, the fastidious nostrils and velvet skin and eyes the color of dark amethysts, the thick, tawny hair. Yet she knew that the search was hopeless.

She got her books and binder and went through all the rooms in the wing, pausing at some length to study the portrait of the young woman reading—that face, Dominique's face, lighted by the candle flame— and to study minutely the ring shining in the fall of lace. There is the ring, there is Mrs. Staynes's ring. And yet that ring is right now on Dominique's finger.

"No," she said aloud, "I don't understand," and went bleakly back to the courtyard.

She waited, trying to get on with her homework. But instead she watched the stone children and how the luminosity was dimming and the sunlight drawing away and leaving the courtyard somber. The stone children had retreated to some private world of their own, and had they been about to speak, would not do so now.

Nina straightened from her hunched position, and to ease her spine, leaned back on stiffened arms and twisted her neck from side to side. Idly then, she picked up the small book that someone had left on the bench and that she had pushed away when she first came. On its cover were the words *The Journal of Odile Chrysostome*. Chrysostome—she knew that name, and Odile, too. Chrysostome had painted Domi's portrait, the one in there in the bedroom, and Odile—Odile was one of these children, but which, she could not remember. She opened the little book to its first page and began reading.

Pontoise
12 JUNE 1802

"My name is Odile, and I am fifteen years of age. This is my first journal. My father keeps one and seems to discover so much pleasure and comfort in it that I am resolved to try to keep one of my own. He says that you do not keep a journal because someone else does, but because you must. He himself keeps his, he says, because of some compulsion to confide a part of himself to the written word. As much of himself, in any case, as can be expressed on paper, where in future time he can return to these confidences and re-experience their pleasures and moods and sorrows, as well as search out the sources of various theories he holds in regard to his art.

"He says that only if you put down at the end of the day what you have seen and felt and thought on that day, can you bring clearly to the page some nearness to truth. If you record only the large events, but neglect those small ones that have struck you for some perhaps unexplainable reason (often it is the small things, he says, that prove most potent for the future), then all precision is lost. A particular shading of sky, the fine edge of reasoning for some decision, the exact words someone spoke, some elusive delicacy of the senses, a turn of emotion, all vanish. We think the memory of them will never escape us, but they are like our dreams, which are often vivid on the moment of awakening, but blurred an hour or two later when only a haunting impression remains.

"Above all, Papa says, if I am as honest as I know how to be, I will discover here as I write, day after day, something of myself, something of my own nature that I might otherwise not be aware of.

"I shall try to be honest, and I might as well begin my honesty by admitting that I have been moved to ask my father for this commonplace book of blank pages because I am filled with glee. K is coming! Upon each occasion I am, as I grow older, increasingly filled with joy at the prospect of seeing him. And after he is gone I wish there were some way I could taste my joy again and recover every word and look of his, his confidences when we go for our long walks through the woods, the stories he tells in the evenings of his travels and the extraordinary people he has met: the grotesque, the weak, the powerful, the purely evil (if such there be), and the chameleons who seem now obscurely evil, now benign. Those like K and my father seem to me to be wholly good, though both are troubled at times, filled with anxieties that are rarely explained except perhaps to each other.

"*K is coming*. Perhaps someday I shall find words shining enough to put beside those three. My family teases me because K is married and is so much older than I. But they have no understanding of me *or* my feelings. He will arrive in—"

A bell rang. And that hard electric warning—the one, single thing Nina disliked in the museum and that seemed to be out of harmony with it—shattered her absorption and gave her a pain in her middle.

"Dominique!" she called again, softly, as before. "I'm here—I've been waiting—where are you? Where have you been? Why don't you come?" She listened in the silence of the courtyard (and the soft splashing of the fountain seemed a part of that silence), listened in the subdued light in which there was no longer bright and dark but only shadow and deeper shadow. As she gathered her books and put them on top of her binder, she heard steps which halted behind her just as she stood up to look and be sure she'd left nothing. She turned, and there was Old Whiskers.

"Hurry up, kid," he said. "Time to get along. You don't wanna get locked up in here."

"I *heard* the bell," Nina said in a sudden fury. "I *heard* it. You can see what I'm doing."

"O.K., O.K.," he said, moving his plump, shiny hands that were so much too small for his body, "no need to get yer dander up. I jus' gotta get everybody outa here."

He followed her as she walked past the fountain and past one of the stone children, a girl. As she went by, "Good night," she whispered, and the child returned her whisper with a smile of infinite meaning. Old Whiskers followed her right into the rotunda, though

[65]

there were other people, she noticed, to be herded out of the château rooms. Leisurely, she went to the Chagall painting and silently said good-bye to it, noted that Mr. Quarles was not at his desk, and without hesitation rejected the idea of asking Old Whiskers what the trouble had been in the museum. Then she crossed to the doors and started for home.

As she ran along the path toward the iron gates she was all at once, for some reason, flooded with happiness and as well with a sense of excited expectation. Yet why expect anything when she had not seen Dominique and might, mystifyingly enough, never see her again? There was no one at home and the apartment would be dark and filled with that revolting smell of mustiness and dust and innumerable meals that always disgusted Nina when she first opened the door and that her mother could not vanquish no matter how long she left the windows open. It was an odor forever soaked into the curtains and carpets and furniture, she said. What, exactly, then, was there to look forward to? Why, Odile's book. There would be the whole, quiet, undisturbed evening to read it in, and she could go to bed whenever she liked.

But when she got to the top of the park and turned to look back at the last sunset light over the sea beyond the Golden Gate, she thought to open the cover of the little book. And there on the flyleaf was pasted a bookplate on which was written *From the library of Victorine Henry*. Nina stood near the bench where she had first met Gil and turned the matter over in her mind.

Old Whiskers didn't like her; he was suspicious of

her; he was keeping an eye on her. Mrs. Henry had, as a matter of fact, still been at the museum, because her door had been opened by someone coming out and Nina, turning away from the painting, had caught a glimpse of her sitting in a remote bloom of lamplight, her head bent over her work. Nina ran back down the hill, across the street where the cable car was going clack-clack-clack-clack, and along past the wall of the museum grounds.

But the museum gates were padlocked and Auguste was just walking away with the ring of keys jingling in his hand. "Auguste!" Nina pronounced it *Oh-goost* as everyone else did. "Auguste, I have a book of Mrs. Henry's I found in the courtyard and I forgot to give it to her. Will you?" She held it out between the bars of the gate.

He came back and gave her a quick look. "Oh, 'allo, it's you." He unlocked the padlock and slipped it out. "Museum's all closed up. You go along over there to my place and put it on the table. Door's open. I'll see she gets it," and he rubbed the palm of his wet hand back and forth over his faded shirt. He'd started the sprinklers going over to the north of the museum entrance and the long, curved jets of water, sweeping back and forth, looked to Nina like dancers turning and turning in the slow movement of a ballet. Auguste swung open the gate, Nina went tearing off across the grass and heard the gate clang behind her.

There was an evening fragrance of flowers and wet grass in the air. The tops of the huge copper beeches, whose heads rose above the roof of the museum, burned Indian red in the last rays of the sun. Perhaps it was the mingling of damp smells, or the look of the trees with caverns of darkness settling in around their feet, or the vast open expanse of lawn surrounding her that brought another burst of happiness swelling up in Nina's chest. She wanted to shout, to run faster than her legs could take her. She was drunk on freedom and space and evening and the vagrant odors of earth. Suddenly the sun's light went from the sky, and the beeches ceased to burn. Flowers in their raked beds were nothing but drifts of paleness.

"Lisabetta!" called someone, faintly, far over to the right of Auguste's cottage.

Nina stopped in order to listen and watch. That had been Dominique. Then she saw Lisabetta streaking from one cave of shadow to another, and behind ran another Lisabetta and beyond darted Dominique, her arms held wide as though she were flying.

"Dominique! Dominique!" Nina's voice rose thinly, seeming to lose itself in this spacious world of dusk and shadows and towering, leafy shapes. She ran toward them, toward the girl and the two cats, and suddenly the second Lisabetta swerved and came racing to meet her. She held out an arm, stooped down as the cat came under her hand, but she touched nothing. It was as though the pale, furry shape possessed no substance, but simply flowed through her fingers like a stream of wind. "You little tricky one!" she cried, chasing after, then laughed and turned at the sound of Dominique calling again. Domi was chasing the Lisabetta Nina had tried to catch, and now she was swooping her up, burying her face in the cat's fur, and letting her go. Then here came the first Lisabetta, and the two cats went careening away, leaping at each other, springing into the air, and then flitting off until they were nothing but two glimmering moths in the dimness.

"Nina, I have something to show you," called Domi, moving away, beckoning, her voice lingering in the quiet air.

"Where have you been?" Nina called back, following her. "I waited."

"I know. I saw you—but old red-face was watching from the library windows, and I thought he might come out. He tells Mrs. Staynes and Mr. Quarles that you talk to yourself—"

"But why would he say that, even though he doesn't like me? I talk to *you*—"

"No need to worry, Nina." Dominique flickered across the grass toward the back of the museum. "He's going on vacation—we'll have two whole weeks—the other guards won't bother—"

Nina saw the tall windows of Mrs. Henry's office flooding light in the shapes of themselves across the shrubbery and the walk underneath them and, as she passed, glimpsed Mrs. Henry at her desk, still working. She rounded the corner of the building and saw Dominique beyond, at the gate that opened into the courtyard. Auguste couldn't have locked it yet because now Dominique disappeared. She had gone in and let it swing closed behind her and Nina, when she came to it, saw her in there, standing near the fountain by one of the stone children, and Nina lifted the latch and went in too. Suddenly Dominique threw back her head and stretched her arms as though trying to touch the sky.

"Look, Nina, look! The color of it—at this time of evening."

Nina tilted her head and gazed at that dome of powerful blue, a blue that almost vibrated because of the jewel green distilled in it. A single star had come out over Mam'zelle's office. "Venus, Dominique. See up there? That's Venus—"

"I know. Come here, Nina. I want to show you something."

Dominique held out her hand, but before Nina could reach her she was kneeling at the side of the flagstones at the base of the smallest stone child, the one near the library doors. She pointed at the earth, and when Nina knelt she saw, in the faint gleam slanting down through leaves from a light still burning in the museum, the small gold circle and reflecting stone of the ring. Incredulously she picked it up. She lifted her eyes and met Dominique's as they knelt there, facing one another at the foot of the statue, but looked down again as Dominique's hand moved forward until their fingertips were within an inch of each other. Dominique's hand was held palm down so that the amethyst of her ring shone.

"There are two Lisabettas, Nina," said Dominique. "Auguste's Lisabetta of your world, that he can hold—or you—but not I. And there is my unearthly Lisabetta that I can hold, but not you. There is my ring that I wear on my finger, but that you could never slip onto yours. And there is that ring, there, the one Mrs. Staynes wears and that I can't touch, though it is mine exactly as this ring on my finger is mine. Unlike the Lisabettas,

Nina, which have never been one and the same, the rings *are* one and the same."

Now Dominique's hand moved again, drifted into Nina's until the rings merged—and were one.

Nina floated for a moment in freezing darkness, then fell forward at the base of the statue. A wandering wind flicked up the pages of her binder, lying open where it had spilled from her arms, and her books and Victorine Henry's *Odile* lay beside it. The evening blue of the sky deepened, the plumes of water in the fountain leaped and splashed. A little yellow-green frog no bigger than a quarter hopped onto Nina's cold hand then hopped off again. But Nina did not move.

Chapter Eight

"—a good hot cup of coffee," Mam'zelle was saying. Her back was turned and she was standing in front of a little kitchen which would ordinarily be hidden behind movable paneling, but now the paneling was pushed back on either side. She was working at a stove, presumably, for she had a kettle and had just poured steaming water into a pot. She waited for a moment or two and suddenly there was a tantalizing fragrance of coffee.

Someone was rubbing Nina's arm, scrubbing away with a very hard palm. Why would anyone do that? She turned her head and saw that it was Auguste; he was seated beside her, leaning over, and she studied the top of his head with its thatch of stiff white hair, and his foreshortened brown leather face marked with long furrows pressed from the corners of his nose right down to the corners of his mouth. And he never noticed that she was watching him and thoroughly taking in her whereabouts: this "richly dark room," she described it to herself, meaning the tones of the wood paneling.

Yet it was filled softly with light from Mam'zelle's desk lamp, a light that made the spines of the books on the walls glow, as well as the colors in the thick carpet —silky reds and blues and greens—and the pale gold of the ceiling that, by reflection, sent down a subdued light of its own.

Mam'zelle turned and was coming toward Nina, who was now aware of herself nestled on a couch whose pillows must have been filled with down, and of a comforter tucked around her. Her shoes were off and she could feel a hot water bottle pressed against the soles of her feet.

"Ah, there you are, child! You've come back," said Mam'zelle. "What a relief! I've called the doctor and he'll be here presently." Auguste shot Nina a look from under his bristle brows, then got up and Mam'zelle took his place. Her hand came out and touched Nina's cheek. "How are you, little one?"

Nina chuckled. "Little one! And I'm taller than you!"

Mam'zelle smiled and nodded. "You are, at that. And I have al-lways so admired an elegant tallness, willowy, like Helena Staynes's. But now I must call your parents at once. Helena told me your name, I think—"

"Nina. Nina Harmsworth. But there's no one at home, Mrs. Henry. They're eating out, and then they're going to a show." Mam'zelle was silent, seeming to take this in. "They don't often, without me—"

"I see. Do you enjoy coffee, Nina?"

"Oh, I'm very fond of it, but I'm not often allowed to have any."

"But perhaps on this occasion," stated Mam'zelle, "you might have a cup. Would you put the pot on the cart, Auguste, and the cups and saucers, and the cream and sugar for Nina? You don't take it straight, do you, child?" Auguste wheeled the cart over and Mam'zelle, dark, firm, small, high-busted, rather slope-shouldered, trim as a plump bird in her bright cherry red, poured and gave round the coffee with an oval hand that bore a big rough gold ring. Nina watched all these infinitely soothing movements and heard the chinking of a bracelet and the click of Mam'zelle's ring on the edges of the saucers. Her chair, over behind the massive desk, Nina noted, was magnificent: a high-backed one, padded all over the inside with dark green leather. "Here, Auguste, sit down now and be comfortable. We shall all be comfortable." Mam'zelle saw that Nina had cream and sugar, offered her and Auguste a plate of cookies, then sipped her own coffee. "*Now!* When you feel ready, Nina, tell us how you came to be found fainted in the courtyard. If Auguste hadn't wondered where you'd got to and come round to lock up the courtyard—and then, on the strength of a hunch, gone in to have a look, I don't know what would have happened to you. Of course, the night watchman—"

Nina stared at Mam'zelle over her cup. "Did I faint? Was that what that was? I've never done it before—"

"We think you fainted. Or perhaps were knocked unconscious. But whether you fell and struck your head, or fainted and then fell, we have no idea. Can you remember?"

Nina frowned. There were things she could tell and

things she could not. At once, her mind closed itself over what could not be told. "I hadn't much lunch, so maybe I was hungry. Or maybe it was finding the ring—"

Mam'zelle's cup clattered in its saucer. "The ring! You found Helena Staynes's ring?"

"Yes," said Nina. "No wonder she was upset. It's down at the foot of the statue, the one of the youngest child, where I fell." She looked at Auguste. "You know my books and binder? Well, it'll be near them. And I have one of yours, Mrs. Henry. About Odile."

"Odile? My *Journal of Odile Chrysostome?* So that's the book you meant, Auguste, the one Nina came back with. Yes, I remember—I had it when Helena and I were with some visitors out there, and then I came in, and I haven't thought of it since. Auguste, you haven't finished your coffee—" He swallowed the last of it, wiped his mouth on the back of his hand, and got up. "The flashlight's in my desk drawer, there at the top left." He went out and they heard his heavy shoes, with their metal toe plates, plocking across the rotunda floor, and there were little resonances after each plock so that you could sense from those small sounds just how high and large and empty the rotunda was. The museum was very still. Presently, far off, they heard Auguste opening one of the library doors. "If it is *only* Helena's ring!" exclaimed Mam'zelle.

"But it is, Mrs. Henry," said Nina in surprise. "It just is."

Mam'zelle studied Nina's face with black, puzzled, excited eyes. "Nina," and she leaned forward, "how did you come to be in the courtyard?" Nina took another sip of coffee then bit into one of the flat, praline-like cookies, full of nuts. "But, of course," and Mam'-zelle leaned back as though satisfied. "You saw the lights in my office and thought you could come in through the courtyard—in through the library—and give me the book yourself instead of leaving it with Auguste."

"I saw your lamp," said Nina faintly. That was true. But she glanced down and away, for by failing to deny what was not true, she had lied as much as if she had spoken a lie. Yet what could be said that would be believed? When she looked up again, there were Mam'-zelle's eyes still on her face.

"What made you faint, Nina? Surely not finding the ring. Or did you stumble and fall against the statue?"

"I'm not sure—exactly." But in her mind she saw clearly that other hand, with its ring stone shining in the light from the museum window, moving into her own hand, until it—*but it couldn't have!* She heard the clatter of her own cup as she made a sudden spasmodic movement of rejection.

"Something frightened you," said Mam'zelle with certainty, "right to the pit of your being." Then there were voices coming along the north corridor and into the rotunda, Auguste's and someone else's. "That will be Dr. Marriot—I phoned him when Auguste carried you in. We have to be certain you're all right before I take you home."

"No!" exclaimed Nina. "Not you, Mrs. Henry—please not you! Couldn't Auguste—"

But Mam'zelle had turned, put down her cup and saucer and got up, and she was holding out her hand as the men came in. "Dr. Marriot, this is Nina Harmsworth." She moved aside so that he could take her chair and a small, elderly man, rather plump like Mam'zelle, with gray hair and very black eyebrows and alert, humorous eyes, came over and sat down and looked at Nina. Lightly he put his hand on her forehead, then leaned over and opened his little bag. Nina saw Auguste put her binder and books on Mam'zelle's desk then take Mrs. Staynes's ring from his pocket and hand it to Mam'zelle. She clasped it between her two palms, nodded triumphantly to Nina, and went to the phone. And you could sense from Mam'zelle's words of affirmation and reply the measure of Helena Staynes's astonished joy at the other end.

Nina had her temperature taken, her eyes peered into, her pulse felt, her knee jerks observed, her heart listened to, and was made to lie flat and bring first the index finger of one hand and then of the other over to her nose to be certain she could aim "right in on the button," said Dr. Marriot.

"That's good," said Nina, smiling at him and feeling perfectly at ease. "Right on the button!" His little joke, or was it a kind of pun? She landed precisely both times. She didn't remember striking herself? She had no pains? No, she said, no pains, and she hadn't struck herself. Just fainted. He gave her a quick double tap on the top of her head with his knuckles as if asking to be let in and assured Mam'zelle that he was quite inclined to believe the fainting was a result of Nina's not having had enough lunch. Of course Nina was to let him know if she fainted again.

After Auguste and Dr. Marriot had gone, Mam'zelle wrapped the amethyst ring in tissue paper and put it in her purse; she would take it to Helena Staynes immediately she had delivered Nina. But Nina, sitting on the edge of the couch, putting on her shoes, was aware of a gray hollow of depression, a sick reluctance at the thought of being delivered. She didn't *want* Mam'zelle taking her home, yet she'd never be allowed to walk there in the dark. In Silverspring, yes; not in San Francisco.

Mam'zelle and Nina went down a hall at the rear of the rotunda to a door which Mam'zelle unlocked, then locked behind them, and which led out to the back of the museum. Mam'zelle's car stood alone in the parking area and as they crossed to it she took Nina's arm.

"Mrs. Staynes tells me some interesting things about you. For instance, that you seriously want to become a curator in a museum. Or was it—not just a curator, but chief curator. I'm intrigued. Though, Nina—" and here Mam'zelle's voice slid down a pitch or two, "you perhaps don't realize the amount of work you have in front of you. Years of study in art history and art criticism, not to speak of anthropology and archaeology —yes, and even chemistry. Actually, that's only the beginning. And you will no doubt change a dozen times before you're twenty. At *least* that—"

"No," said Nina. "No, I don't think I will, Mrs. Henry. I can remember the smell of the Silverspring Museum even now from when I was four and what I felt about it—that it was an absolutely special place. I always loved it, and after a while, when I got older, Mrs. Bourne sometimes let me help—she let me sweep and dust. And just before we had to leave Silverspring, she was beginning to let me type labels on a big typewriter because I'm careful, and now and then she even let me help put things in the cases. Once when I was by myself doing this, I got my Museum Feeling. I mean, holding the things the pioneers had made and some of the old things they'd brought from wherever they came from, it was as if there wasn't any time at all between their lives and mine." Nina's voice faded and her face went hot in spite of a chill little wind blowing across the lawns. "It's hard to explain. I don't know —it must seem silly and childish when I say it like that—"

"No," said Mam'zelle. They had reached her car and she fitted the key into the lock. "Not at all. I believe you could even say that I had a Museum Feeling once." She opened the door and Nina went round and, when Mam'zelle flipped up the catch, got in on the other side. "I haven't told many people," Mam'zelle said. "Only Helena Staynes and one or two others."

One day, she said, after her husband died and she had decided to house their huge art collection in a museum which she would dedicate to his memory, she had come here from France to look at some property her husband had owned for many years.

"I fell in love with San Francisco," she said, "its hilliness, its air, its incredible views, its streets plunging down to the water. And the day I came up here I felt almost feverish with excitement. The homes over there on the other side of the street, opposite where the museum stands now, hadn't been destroyed in the 1906 earthquake and were being perfectly cared for, but the apartment houses on this side, jammed tight together in typical San Francisco fashion, seemed to me very ordinary and unattractive so that I knew I'd have no regrets in tearing them down. But I loved the street itself, the atmosphere of it, especially because of the trees—there was even something slightly Parisian about it. And suddenly as I stood there on the sidewalk my feeling came to me.

"There's a building in Paris, Nina, called the Ministry of Marine, that extends an entire block in the Place de la Concorde. All at once that was the building I saw in front of me, but smaller, changed to be right for these grounds, still elegant, still noble, with wings on either side, yet not awesome—not more than two stories—with gardens where people could walk.

"I've said that that was the building I saw in front of me. And I don't mean I suddenly imagined it. I mean, I *saw!*" Mam'zelle sent out the word "saw" with such possessed, piercing intensity that for the third time that day, the hairs lifted along the backs of Nina's arms. "The apartment houses were no longer there; they had simply vanished and my golden museum built of French stone stood before me.

"I can remember to this day, to this very moment, how my eyes traveled leisurely over its entire length, taking in with the utmost peace and contentment every detail, watching the movements of Auguste working away at one of the flower beds—I was hoping he'd come with me from my home in Paris. I watched cloud shadows passing over, people going up the steps onto the loggia, and the tall dark green doors opening and closing." Mam'zelle paused as if recalling exactly how it had been.

"A sort of vision, was it, Mrs. Henry?"

"Yes," said Mam'zelle. "Yes, I suppose it was. And I had it standing right out there in the street, at midday, with the traffic passing and children skating by. That was forty years ago. I think Jules would be pleased. Jules Henri—Ahn-ree—that was my husband's name, the way we say it in France, not Henry as they call it in this country."

"Jules," repeated Nina, pronouncing it *Z-zhule* just as it had fallen on her ear, then *Ahn-ree*, and *Frah-nce*, almost losing the "n" in each word, but sounding it slightly against her palate as Mam'zelle had done.

"Ex-cellent!" exclaimed Mam'zelle. "You'll have your languages in no time. You are a little parrot. And if you're to be a curator of the first order, you must have several languages—French, Italian, Spanish, German," said Mam'zelle, clicking them off with her ring on the rim of the wheel. "I wonder if—" but she shook her head. "Who knows what will happen, let alone before summer vacation." Nina gazed at her. What had she meant, "*let alone* before summer vacation"? "Did you take in all I said about what you must study in order to become a curator? Those special subjects that are only a beginning?"

"Yes," said Nina. "Yes, I did. And I can be starting my languages next year—and my art." She was exalted. "I'll be learning about all those people like the man who painted *Time Is a River Without Banks*, won't I?"

"Yes, Nina, you will—" and Mam'zelle laughed suddenly, but not at her, Nina felt. Not at her! Then they were both laughing as if out of some general joyousness and camaraderie, even as Mam'zelle was driving her home up this dark, barren, looming street with its clutter of old cars run in across the sidewalk.

"Here," Nina said all at once. And her joy left her.

Mam'zelle parked, turning her car in where there was a space, then gathered up her purse which was more like a satchel. "I'm coming in with you," she said.

"No, Mrs. Henry—*please*. It's all right—"

"I must, child. The halls will be dark—"

"But they're so ugly!" cried Nina desperately.

Mam'zelle sat quiet, looking at her. "Nina, you need have no pride with me, believe me. And I will not leave you until I have you safe in your own apartment."

Upstairs in the dim hall at the apartment door, Nina unlocked it then turned on the light inside, struggling painfully with herself about inviting Mam'zelle in. Mam'zelle opened her satchel-like purse and took out a little book. "The *Odile Chrysostome* for you to read in bed tonight. Will you accept it from me—a gift? I think it belongs to you; it's just right for you." Nina took it and held it against her chest, staring at Mam'zelle in astonishment, and before she could say a word Mam'zelle had reached out and tapped her on the cheek. "As for the courtyard," she said, "*c'est un mystère*, Nina, *c'est un grand mystère*." Then she turned and went off along the hall, and at the top of the stairs she paused to send Nina a last wave of the hand.

"Good night, Mam'zelle. Good night. Thank you!"

Nina read steadily with complete absorption until ten-thirty, then, having left the light on in her parents' bedroom, turned off the one at the end of the couch and curled down. I'll dream about Odile or Dominique. I'll dream about the courtyard, and the unearthly Lisabetta, and the ring, and Dominique's hand—

But though she dreamed, Dominique had no part in it. She was in a long, narrow hall that had a high ceiling. The woodwork was white and the walls were covered with an old-fashioned but very beautiful moss-green and white figured wallpaper. There was a dark green rug on the floor—a silky rug like Mam'zelle's, silky and thick—that went up the stairs on her right. To the side of the stairway there was an enormous window reaching up two stories that let in a broad fall of sunlight. And there were ferns and all sorts of flowering plants grouped thickly in a brass planter along the base of the broad windowsill. Someone—she thought it must be Helena Staynes—was saying something behind her and now the voice went wandering off into the room on the left of the hall. Nina was standing at the foot of the stairs looking up. There were children of different ages on the stairs, three girls and three boys, running up the stairs ahead of her, calling to each other, and presently they disappeared along the hall on the upper floor, still laughing and calling, as though finding treasures they wanted everyone to share.

Of course! They were the stone children of the courtyard. "Chiro! Gabrielle! Cyprian!" And then, "Odile!" they cried.

"No," said the one who must be Odile, the last to have run up the stairs, and she was still visible to

Nina, standing looking at something hidden from Nina's sight. "Wait a minute, because first I want Nina to see something. She *must* see it—hurry, Nina!"

Eagerly Nina started up, and the fresh, damp smell of ferns and of watered earth was in her nostrils. Her feet sank into the softness of the carpet; she noted how its pile shone in the leaf-caught, moving patches of sunlight. Then Odile turned and leaned over the banister in the upper hall, and her alive, glowing, triumphant face was the face of the child in the courtyard at whose feet Dominique had pointed out Mrs. Staynes's ring.

But no sooner had Nina reached the second floor and was holding out her hand to meet Odile's so that they could go off together, than the whole scene ceased to exist. Nina lay there wide awake, desperately trying to get it back, the life of it, the intense reality, as though her entire happiness depended upon it, but it was gone—vanished forever. What did she want me for? What did she want me to see? Now I'll never know. And Nina was flooded with sorrow, with a most poignant and bitter sense of loss.

Chapter Nine

" 'Saytoon meestair—saytoon gr-rand meestair.' That's what Mrs. Henry said, the woman who owns the museum." French, for some reason, Nina decided, felt extremely satisfying on her tongue. "What does it mean, Dad?"

Her father, drinking his leisurely Saturday morning coffee, looked at her, gave her his slight, sweet smile that just slightly deepened the wrinkles at the corner of his eyes. Those little wrinkles stayed there, as if he were always about to smile, which he did sometimes, but rarely laughed. "It's a mystery," he said. "It's a great mystery. That's what it means. And *what* was a mystery, Nina?"

She was silent, and then, "Do you believe in ghosts, Dad? In spirits?"

"I'm not sure. The British do, it seems to me, much more than we in this country. Perhaps it's because of the antiquity of their buildings, something we don't have, but even the most modest householders will have their ghost stories that they believe in quite firmly."

She felt his eyes on her, and presently, "Is it the museum? Are you afraid to go back?"

"Dad, can you love and fear something both at the same time?"

"Of course, Squirrel. Just as you can both love and hate, the way you did me when we left Silverspring."

Her head came up and in an instant she had shoved back her chair and her arms were around him. "I didn't, Dad—I didn't!" She hugged him with passion. "I'm so glad you're still here, that you didn't die—"

He looked up at her, his fingers grasping her arm. "Know what you know, Nina. Confess to yourself—it's better that way, less wearing." And meeting his eyes, she knew perfectly well what the truth was: not that she had wanted him to die, but that she *had* hated him while at the same time, deep underneath, she loved him and could never stop loving him no matter what else she felt. Yet how can a person feel two opposite things at once! But she had—and did now, about Dominique: fear, or more nearly terror, and yet just as deeply a very powerful attraction that was far more compelling than mere fascination. Perhaps this, in its own way, was a kind of love.

The phone rang and Mrs. Harmsworth said it was Helena Staynes asking for Nina. She wanted to express her gratitude.

"But why did you wear the ring, Mrs. Staynes, knowing it was too big?"

"Because of the purple suit—and visitors coming."

"Auguste or Philippe would have found it eventually."

"If it hadn't been dug under and lost forever. But I

could swear I looked around the base of the statue near the library. I remember standing there, talking."

"The statue of Odile, you mean." It was not a question, but a statement.

There was a pause, and then, "We don't know which one she is, Nina. Chrysostome never put any names on the bases, and because of differences in style, we believe they were carved at different times so that we have no idea of the ages of the children in relation to each other."

"Oh," said Nina, not understanding. "Well, that one *is* Odile." She was lost in a clear recollection of her dream, of that moment when Odile had called out, "I want Nina to see this. She *must* see it," and then had turned and leaned over the railing in the upper hall. The others had called her Odile and she had answered.

"But how can you be sure, Nina? I don't believe anyone else is, not to my knowledge. None of the paintings of her as a child show her clearly, though there're portraits of some of the others in the family." There was a questioning silence on the other end of the line.

Nina held her breath, for she had a little quick notion, without need to reason it out, that if she spoke of her dream and of the children, she might be led into telling about Dominique who, in the courtyard one day, had called them all by their names. This she remembered now with perfect certainty.

"Nina?"

"Yes, Mrs. Staynes, I'm here. I've been thinking. And maybe it's because of the journal—Odile's journal. Mrs. Henry gave it to me and I've been reading it.

Maybe I want that statue to be Odile because it's my favorite."

"There's a volume two," Helena Staynes said, "but Mrs. Henry has it only in French. We must try to get it for you in English—now that you've begun to know Odile."

Chapter Ten

Nina had finished the journal Sunday night. And because she couldn't bear it to be finished, started all over again, seeing ever more deeply into Odile and into her feelings for K. But now she was surer than ever that only Cyprian and Gabrielle had been mentioned, Odile's most loved brother and sister, and that she had been right in her instinct not to speak of her dream. For how could she know, even in a dream, the names of children no earthly person had told her?

On Monday, when Nina was in the auditorium waiting for assembly to begin, Gil came down the aisle, hesitated for a moment, and then sat down abruptly in the seat next to her. "Why're you so interested in that painting by Chagall in the entrance hall—at the museum, I mean? Mrs. Staynes told me."

She reflected. "I don't know," she said slowly. "I just am—I like it."

"Is that all?" he persisted, fixing her with his fiery blue-green eyes. "*Why* do you like it?"

"I guess because of its strangeness. It's like a fairy

tale where anything could happen and you'd believe it." He smiled a little but did not answer. "Mother and Dad and I went to the museum yesterday," she went on. "They'd never been, and when Mother looked at the painting she said she couldn't understand why Chagall had painted it. She said it was like an insane dream, and how could anyone know what it meant. But Dad said that though it's like a dream, to him it's full of meaning even if he can't quite express what the meaning is. He thinks Chagall may be right, that time *is* a river without banks."

"And do you?" Gil asked.

Nina turned to him. Now his head was down and he was picking away at the spine of his binder and she noticed the queer designs he'd drawn all over the faded blue cover. "I don't know. I've never thought—"

"You've never *thought!*" He looked round at her in pure exasperation. "Well, what was all that about your museum feeling, then—in those rooms you were talking about?"

"But I don't understand. What's my Museum Feeling got to do with the painting?"

Gil sighed as if burdened, slumped down in his seat, propped an elbow on the arm of it, and leaned his head on his hand. "But of course the thing is," he mused, "when a person's gone as far as I have, he prob'ly expects too much. And then I'll bet you don't ever really think anyway."

She stared at him, and saw the corner of his mouth twitch, saw it quiver. He was teasing her. But all the same,

[90]

"What do you mean, I don't really think! I'm *always* thinking—"

"No, you're not," he said lightly, matter-of-factly. "The truth is, you're just messing around. You're just vaguely mulling things over, dredging them up, and you know it. That's not thinking—the kind that goes from step to step—"

"The kind you do, no doubt."

He chuckled. "Yep, the kind I do—sometimes." He considered. "Anyhow, it doesn't matter." He straightened suddenly, bringing up one knee ahead of the other so that his binder, being tilted, flipped open, and Nina glanced down, her eye caught by color, and there was Chagall's painting—a reproduction—pasted on one of the pages. Instantly Gil clapped his binder to, and Nina looked up at him and they studied one another, and there was a challenge in his eyes, but not at all anything shutting out—welcoming, rather.

"So that's it," she said softly. "So that's your project—Time." She knew it as surely as if the word were written on his forehead or inside her own. And why this fact, the knowledge of Gil's project, should somehow excite her, she had no idea. Possibly it was her imagination that was kindled, for she saw all at once the connection between her Museum Feeling and the painting. "Time is a river without banks"—yes, immeasurable and indefinable. And she understood, with no need for words, that it was the paradox and, somehow, the sadness of Time that drew her to the possessions of those long gone: objects, unthinking, unfeeling objects that yet have their own voices, and that outlast the loving flesh that created them. And she understood, too, that it was the inexplicable quality of Time that had probably drawn Gil, challenged him and forced him to come to grips with it. But had he ever felt its sadness, she wondered, something that for her had nothing to do with gloom or despondency. "It's true, isn't it, Gil?" He did not answer. "I won't say anything, any more than you would about my Feeling. Shall I promise?"

He looked at her for a moment, then shook his head. "If you wanted to, you'd let it slip. But you won't. And it probably makes no difference anyway—to anybody but me, I mean."

Their eyes held one another's so long that had they felt less communion they might have been embarrassed. As it was, they rested in that mutual exchange with complete ease and unselfconsciousness, then their gazes fell away and Nina, until Gil spoke again, lapsed into her private world where thought and imagination mingled and she did not know where one left off and the other began.

She hadn't quite decided if it was to test herself concerning Dominique and the possibility of seeing her again that she had turned toward the park after school. Marny and two of her friends were sitting on the grass near the bench, not noticing her as she approached, not looking round. And as Nina came opposite them, she glanced down and saw Gil's binder lying among theirs. She knew it at once because of the unmistakable drawings on the cover and along the ragged, picked-at spine. Yet it wasn't possible he could be here because he had hurried past her as she left school, running up the stairs and going in, seeming wholly absorbed in some overwhelming concern of his own. She knew he hadn't seen her.

She stood for a moment, reflecting. Were the girls expecting him, waiting for him? Considering the extreme privacy, as far as Gil was concerned, of the contents of his notebook, the fact that it should be lying here was incongruous. How had they come by it?

Marnychuck turned suddenly and studied her, and that other park scene apparently came back. "Well," she said, "if it isn't something-in-a-museum." Nina went over and dropped cross-legged into that inimical circle, while Marny took her in with appraising, wordly eyes. When Nina, with a touch of awe, had first described Marnychuck to her father, he had said, "Yes, she's one of the old ones. They've never had any childhood and they're on to everything. Age has nothing to do with it." Marny lifted an eyebrow. "Why so friendly all of a sudden? You need something?"

Nina's hands went cold. "Not really—"

"If you're looking for Gil," said Marny, "he isn't here—as you may have noticed." There was an explosion of mirth from the other two, but Marny's expression never changed. "He's probably still at school, chasing all over trying to remember where he's been." She grinned suddenly, and the others shrieked with joy, and Nina understood at once that they had taken Gil's binder and that Gil didn't know who had taken it or if anyone had. "Oh, shut up," said Marny, but the two paid no attention. "Are you and Gil pretty good friends? You seemed to be this morning."

"I don't really know him. Do you?"

"Who doesn't? Going around the way he does, talking to himself and squinting up his eyes and always writing things." Marny chuckled, no doubt at the thought of what she'd been reading, and the sound gave Nina a turn, coming from that lean face, that flat, unhappy mouth.

"When a person's gone as far as I have—" Gil had said. What could he have meant by that? Gone into himself? Thought his way in, or into the subject that fascinated him? Did he accept that he wasn't like the others, that they positively disliked him, that he was thought an insufferable oddity? Yet he was the one person she had met to whom she could say exactly what she felt. He asked her abrupt, direct questions in a way she liked, and she could answer, not with evasion for the sake of what he would think, but with the truth, no matter how out of the way it might seem.

" 'What are you do-ing, may I ask, Gilbert Patrick?' " intoned one of the girls in a high, mocking voice. " 'I'm *think*-ing, Mrs. Trotter.' 'And what are you *think-ing*, may I ask, Gilbert Patrick?' 'I'm sorry, Mrs. Trotter, but that's my private business—' "

Marny's friends were about to go off into shouts of hilarity again when there came a piercing whistle from the path farther down, and the girls got up to go and have a look. When a conversation began with the whistler, Marny got up too, lazy and casual, and joined the others, pushing them apart and leaning her elbows on their shoulders so as to take command of the situation.

At once Nina reached over, caught up Gil's binder,

tucked it under her own and got up and walked away neither quickly nor slowly, so that to anyone glancing round it would have appeared only that she knew she wasn't wanted. She controlled herself until she reached the bend in the path leading down the museum side of the park, that stretch she had raced down ahead of Gil when he'd first told her of the French Museum, and he had taken it as a challenge and caught up with her and passed her. But Nina ran now as she would never have been able to run then, for she was filled with an electrifying mixture of glee and terror, glee because she knew that none of the girls could catch up with her, and terror because the whistler had been a boy. If he overtook her she would not give up the notebook without a struggle: the kind of uncaring, mindless struggle she could enter into whenever she was swept by fury.

She ran without looking back until she was in the middle of the first block beyond the cable car tracks, then tossed a glance over her shoulder. And there they were, Marny and the two girls and the boy, standing together at the top of the path where it emerged from cover, and they were coolly watching her, as if with amusement, then Marny said something and they all burst out laughing and turned and went up and disappeared.

What did they mean to do? Nina stopped at a drugstore to ask the way to the address that Gil had printed on the cover, then ran all the way for fear Marny and her friends should have rounded back through the park and along behind the museum to come out ahead of her. On that long avenue, sloping downhill from where the museum stood, she had no idea whether or not she had been seen before she could turn onto Gil's street and find his number, which was the fourth from the corner. Two anxious rings of the bell, and footsteps were heard and the door opened and a woman looked at her. She was Nina Harmsworth, she said, mortified to hear her voice shake, for she was still out of breath. She had Gil's binder, she said. It had been stolen.

"Stolen!" repeated Mrs. Patrick. "But what on earth for, I wonder. Come in, dear." She held out her hand and slid it along Nina's shoulders as she stepped inside. "I've been out shopping and only just now got back. I'd no time for lunch so I'm giving myself a cup of tea and some toast in front of the fire."

"Oh, am I *lucky*!" breathed Nina, then smacked her hand over her mouth. "I didn't mean the toast—I meant that you're here!"

Mrs. Patrick laughed and led the way into the living room. "But Gil always has something to eat when he gets home and so must you. It's only natural—on top of all that running."

Nina went to the couch and Mrs. Patrick took Gil's binder from her. It's nice, all this, Nina thought, absorbing the room, her eyes skimming, not staring at anything directly. It was exactly what she and her mother and father would have liked, something comfortable and roomy, with plenty of books and magazines and pictures, and the fireplace with a fire going. Imagine that—a fireplace in an apartment! She hadn't thought it possible, but how did you find an apartment like this? It was probably horribly expensive, and they would never—her own family—be able to afford anything like it. Not now. Not for a long, long time.

"Who was it stole Gil's binder, Nina? Do you know?" And Nina told her about the park, leaving out Marnychuck's remarks about him, and the others' mockery of him. "Pointless," said Mrs. Patrick. "Stupid and pointless. I'll just put another log on and make more tea and we'll have it together." And when she had settled opposite Nina, "Are you in Gil's class? I don't remember you. Are you new?"

She'd just come, Nina said. She took a bite of the hot toast, oozing butter right to the edges, and Mrs. Patrick moved the bowl of strawberry jam over, and asked if she was making friends. She knew some of the girls, she said, and had lunch with them sometimes, but friends—that was different. But then she'd only been here four months.

"Four months!" repeated Mrs. Patrick ironically. "Well, it's all according to the kind of person you are, isn't it? Do you mind—I mean, not making friends easily? Are you lonely?"

Nina shook her head. She'd never minded being alone, she could never remember having been lonely up at Silverspring. If some friend hadn't been with her after school, she would talk to Windy when he came to meet her. He had had to be left with the Hudsons because it would have been cruel to bring him to an apartment in the city, a cat who loved to run in the wind, up over the hills, through the woods. They'd go out into the woods together in the early morning when everything smelled sharper than at any other time. Then at dusk, when any little moving shadow might be a mouse or a mole and there were cracklings and stirrings, he'd go mad. Again and again he would hide, then leap out just as she passed him and go tearing ahead, his feet drumming like a little horse's on the path, disappear for five minutes as if he'd deserted her, then there he'd be around a bend, one front paw up as if to say, "Well, where've you been? I've had to stop here, fiddling around and wasting the evening while I waited for you—"

Mrs. Patrick smiled to herself as she drank her tea. "Yes, I can see him, standing there waiting—"

She missed Windy, Nina said, and going off into the hills with him after dinner, and then it would begin to get dark and the lights would come on here and there in the trees. You couldn't walk in the city after dark, but why would anybody want to?

"Nobody would," said Mrs. Patrick, "though we used to seven or eight years ago. It's sad."

There was an easy calmness about her, Nina decided, that made her very unlike her own mother who, even in the hills when she had been home all day, would never have taken time to sit down in the middle of the afternoon and indulge herself in a cup of tea, what with the housework, she would say, and the vegetable garden and her husband sick and having to be taken care of. She never sat down all day long. She would show you the dustpan. "Look at that!" she'd exclaim. "And I swept only yesterday morning. Where does it all come from? No peace for the wicked!" It was a thing she often said.

"Mother's always at me about friends. I don't know why—you can't *make* yourself."

"No," said Mrs. Patrick, "you can't. Not if you're one of the solitaries—but mostly happy that way."

"Dad says when we're older, it gets better. It did for him. He was sick and out of school when he was a boy, but later he found his own kind."

Mrs. Patrick studied Nina and Nina thought how she had Gil's absorbing gaze, only hers was not so demanding, so piercing, and her eyes were dark. "Are you Gil's friend?" Mrs. Patrick asked suddenly.

Nina smiled at that. "I don't know. I hadn't thought. Maybe I am—now."

There was silence, and then a key rattled, the front door opened and closed, and Nina saw Gil beyond the living room arch starting to go past without looking in.

"Gil, Nina brought your binder."

He stood there staring at them, and Nina got up and took it to him and thought how his eyes were now even more startling in color in contrast to his white face. But even as he took the binder, she saw relief flooding him. He did not smile, only grasped it in both hands then looked at her.

"That's the last thing I'd have thought of in a million years—you and the notebook here together."

Chapter Eleven

He had months and months of notes on his project in this binder, he said, coming in and sitting down, and Mrs. Patrick went out to make toast for him. It was all a mixture of things he'd copied and things he'd written down whenever he had even half an idea, no matter how crazy it was, and when there got to be too much, he'd file away those pages and put in fresh. If he'd lost what he had here, he could never have gotten any of it back, never remembered. But how could those kids have known that?

Mrs. Patrick came in and put down his plate and a cup of coffee and he spread the toast thickly with jam and began eating. "It's just that they've always got to have some little thing going," he said presently, almost musingly, "some stupid little kick, no matter how senseless. They give me a pain in the rump." Mrs. Patrick chuckled and Nina, slipping him a sideways glance, noticed how clearly his freckles stood out, stains spattered across his thin face, a face that in its thinness made him seem older than he must surely be. For a fraction of a second, she knew exactly how he must appear to those others, with his secret intensity, his fierce way of looking at a person, obliviously, so that the other, some stranger to his kind, could only be made to feel uncomfortable, unnecessary, insulted. Yes, he was odd! But not insufferable, the way they must see him. To her, quite the opposite.

She looked up and Mrs. Patrick's eyes were on her, calm, faintly smiling, as though there were all the time in the world or as if time, inside this room, inside this particular moment, were held in abeyance and no one need say a word. Gil was watching the fire, his anger seemingly past, for all at once he leaned back and had a good long stretch, then let out a contented sigh. Nina heard the fire flapping and how it would creak when the wood shifted. She was aware of the quiet, of her own happiness as usually she was not, in the midst of it, but only later when she looked back and it was gone.

Gil sat up, finished his coffee, then reached out and touched Nina's knee with the point of his finger. "Would you care to see a sort of messy room?"

It had two large windows giving a view of the bay, a thoroughly used room, every corner of it: very personal and expressive of Gil, Nina thought. There was a good-sized desk, well littered, and half a wall of bookshelves, completely filled. A large, sloping pillow, the kind used for reading in bed, had been tossed on the floor. The bedside table was an unusually large one whose surface around the lamp base was entirely covered with reading matter piled at random with innumerable slips of paper sticking out at the edges. A shelf underneath was in the same condition. Piles of magazines, notebooks, paper-backs, and letters were stacked along whatever wall space was available, together with a number of file boxes packed with cards interspersed with subject indicators.

There were four signs on the walls, apparently printed by Gil. The one over the desk said,

Time is ʳhe ghost of space.
—HENRI BERGSON

and the one between the windows,

I must hear from thee every day in the hour,
For in a minute there are many days.
—WILLIAM SHAKESPEARE

and the one near the door,

The scientist lives as close to mystery
and wonder as the poet or artist.

—DAD

and the one over the bed,

What lies on the edge of perception, from
where anyone might come moving in, not
necessarily from our layer of time?

—LONNY

It made Nina catch her breath—that last one, as it had not the first time she'd heard Gil say those words, for then, the whole experience of Dominique was still to come. She was standing by the bed, looking up. "This is what you said—"

"I know. It's what I said that time we got to talking

up at the top of the park about so many children dying in the early days, and I said that that wasn't all there was to it. I remember exactly. I thought you were a darned unusual girl."

Nina felt her face change color. She didn't know what to make of him: his way of, unexpectedly like this, coming out with precisely what he thought. Lonny, she knew now, was what he called his mother, and though she had never up at Silverspring heard any mother called by her first name, she liked it. It seemed in Gil's case companionable and right and not in the least cool or presumptuous. She went over and sat on the arm of an easy chair, repeating to herself, "What lies on the edge of perception—" And it occurred to her that Gil might understand about Dominique, that one day she might confess to him and be brought to feel that Dominique's hand merging into her own was in fact not as terrifying and unbearable a happening as something primitive, atavistic in her had made her body believe. "Your father, Gil—would *he* think that anyone might come moving in?"

He considered. "I'm not sure about that. Dad's a physicist, but even so I do know he not only believes in mysteries but that maybe some are going to have to stay that way. When Lonny reads poetry out loud, he says it gives him notions that might not have anything to do with the poem. What I mean is, he likes little strange sideways glimpses—ideas that won't go into formulas."

"But 'Time is the ghost of space.' I don't get that," Nina said. "How can it be? Why should it be?"

Gil was hunched up, cross-legged on the bed, and he

frowned at her for a second. "It can be," he said, "because space is something real—it exists—but time is only in our heads. Just as there have to be bodies for there ever to be ghosts—or, you could say, shadows— of them, so there has to be space for us to have an idea there is such a thing as time, space for objects to take time to move in, change in, because everything *does* change. No space, no time."

"I get it on top," Nina said after a bit, "but not deep underneath."

"Do you really, Nina?" Lonny Patrick said from the doorway. "I don't think I do—get it on top, I mean. Gil," she said, "it's almost five-thirty. What about Nina—"

Nina jumped. "Oh, I'll never get home by six—never! Could I phone? My mother leaves work at five-thirty—oh, if only she hasn't—"

"But, Nina, we want you to stay for dinner and we'll drive you home." Mrs. Patrick led the way to the study. "No," she said, glancing in, "it's only twenty past, so you're all right. But you ask about staying." She went off and Nina heard her, presently, clashing pots in the kitchen and then the front door closed.

"It's a good idea—your staying," Gil said as he went by. "Dad's arrived. I'll be up front."

Nina saw his father standing in the hall, a big solid man with red hair, much lighter than Gil's. He and Mrs. Patrick were just going into the living room, then she heard his and Gil's voices and Dr. Patrick was teasing him about something and Gil tossed the teasing back, and there was a tone in their voices as if they liked each other and were glad to see one another.

Feeling incredibly overtaken by unexpected events, Nina sat for a moment with her hand on the phone. "I am in Gil's house," she said softly aloud, "and I am being planned on to stay for dinner." Then she dialed the bookstore.

He wanted, Gil told her at dinner, to someday write the hugest, most inclusive book that had ever been written about Time, a book that would explain the whole business, he said.

"Mmm. Nobel prize material—that sort of thing, I assume," Dr. Patrick observed, sending Nina a dry little gleam of the eye.

"We-ell, maybe not Nobel *prize*," Gil admitted modestly. "Maybe not the *whole* business about Time. I suppose only God could do that. But I mean everything so far known to man." Part of his project, he said, had to do with prophetic dreams, because that was where the proof lay of a belief he had about Time. He'd never heard anyone else speak of this proof, or read it anywhere, and he was asking all his relatives and friends of the family to write down their dreams for him.

"I know of a prophetic dream," Nina said, "but I can't tell it to you because it isn't mine to tell, and only part of it has turned out so far." She was seeing Dominique crouched in the shadowy corner of her wall bed in the little bedroom in the museum, and then, later, hearing her, "I see you, in my childhood dream, standing at the door, and the lightning flashes, and my father is standing behind you. *I see him*. And there is some connection between you."

[105]

"But *what* part of the dream has turned out, Nina?" demanded Gil in enormous excitement. "*What* part? *Why* can't you tell?"

"I can't—that's all. I just can't. I shouldn't have brought it up. But there's one I've had that I keep thinking about." And she told them her dream of the narrow house and the hall with its high ceiling and long, curved stairway, and Mrs. Staynes going into a room somewhere behind her, still talking, and the children calling, and one of them looking down over the balustrade above her, telling her to come up—come up and see something. But what that something was, Nina did not know, and now she would never know. It had been so real, so clear, that dream, every detail of it still printed in her mind. She could get back even now the smell of the damp earth in the planter and the wet leaves and flowers.

"Write it all out, Nina, and give it to me," said Gil, "and I'll put it in my dream file under Harmsworth, Nina—"

But even as he spoke, Nina all at once put her hands up and covered her face, for something had come to her and she wanted to feel it again, to try to get back whatever it was hovering on the edge of memory. "I've just thought. I wasn't alone on the stairs. I mean, the children were there in front of me at different levels, running up and calling. But there was someone, I'm sure, just behind me at my elbow. I felt the person touch my elbow without saying a single word. How strange that I've only just now remembered, and I've thought of that dream so many times."

Nina was, of course, filled with apprehension and depression on the way home. But Gil had his head down and he was whistling while they got out of the car and Nina said good-bye to the Patricks, and he never once looked around. Suddenly, as they crossed the street, he shoved his hands in his pockets and looked up at the sky. "All summer!" he said. "I've got all summer!" He'd talked to Mrs. Staynes on the corner last night and she had said there was a book in the museum library about Picasso, explaining why he showed all sides of a model's face at once. It was because of Einstein's theories about space and time. And this had to do, too, she'd said, with a painting by a man named Marcel Duchamp called *Nude Descending a Staircase* that showed the figure in a different position on each step so that you weren't getting one second of time in the painting but the entire descent at a single glance. "You see how there isn't any end to my project? Now there's this whole painting angle I have to go into, and all the books I need are right there at the museum. Why, I could go on for the rest of my life just—"

"But, Gil, how're you to earn a living?"

"Oh, I don't know," he said vaguely, happily. "Some way, I guess, I won't need much money."

And she thought, after he had gone, how there had been no need for apprehension. For he hadn't noticed the street or the shabby old buildings, nor ever once given a look to the hall they went along, nor the stairs. She had an idea he would never notice things like that.

Chapter Twelve

It was a week before Nina's fear of Dominique was overcome by the desire to see her and to hear again that husky voice with its rich "r's." But on the day she finally chose to go to the museum, Dominique was not to be found.

Auguste was in the courtyard setting out five-finger ferns and maidenhair in the moist, black, shaded earth, and until he should be finished and Dominique might come, Nina folded herself down, cross-legged, on the flagstones to watch his quick fingers. Presently a furry side was pressed against her arm, and Lisabetta's head poked in under her elbow. She surveyed Nina's lap, stepped delicately in, curled down and settled herself. Nina stroked the creamy back with its faint markings and Lisabetta lifted a pale gray face.

" 'Allo, *p'tite*," said Auguste. "Where 'ave you been, you bad cat? Birding?"

"What does *p'tite* mean, Auguste?"

" 'Little one.' Did you know 'ow I got 'er? Mrs. Staynes see 'er in a pet shop, this little strange pussy-cat with the Siamese body and the tabby face and legs and tail. An' she think—why, she is almost *exactement* like the Lisabetta of the young Dominique, an' so we will 'ave a museum cat an' we will call her Lisabetta after that other one. This little one is made for us! So she bring 'er to me to keep, jus' a tiny kitten, 'an ever since, she an' me, we stay together. She is my girl, *n'est-ce pas*, Lisabetta?" Lisabetta blinked at him in a bliss of comfort and warmth and opened her mouth in answer but made no sound.

"But, Auguste, how could Mrs. Staynes know that Dominique's cat was named Lisabetta?"

Auguste returned her stare of surprise.

"You mean you 'aven't seen the painting? Go an' look for yourself. It is over there—over beyond Mam'-zelle's office at the corner of the other wing, a big roomful of paintings by Chrysostome. 'E is the one who carve all these children."

"Yes, I know." Nina lifted Lisabetta and put her in a patch of sun, where she began washing herself.

A few minutes later Nina was standing at the entrance of a long, airy, high-ceilinged gallery over whose arch were fixed letters and figures in silver metal, *Jean Louis Baptiste Chrysostome, 1742–1805.* Her eyes took in the whole softly lighted room, its pale walls lined with small and large paintings in gold frames, and she felt that she was about to take another step toward some final knowledge of the true nature of Dominique who had been painted as a child by a man who had lived two hundred years ago.

She entered the gallery, looking quickly from painting to painting with their scarlets, their powerful blues and greens and umbers, until, walking down the center, she saw Dominique's face at the far end, the eyes steadily watching her approach, and in Domi's arms was Lisabetta. She went forward and read the sign, *Dominique de Lombre with Her Cat, Lisabetta.* This Dominique of the painting could be no more than eleven or twelve at the most, wholly young, fresh, untried, for whom anything was possible, any joyous triumph. And though at first Nina had taken Dominique to be near her own age, she had come to sense that the girl was possessed of realms of knowledge and emotion she herself had no conception of. What age could she be: the Domi she had talked with, who had asked for her help and to be her friend, who combined in herself this child of the painting, holding her pet, the center of her own universe, and, at the same time, the essence of that young woman, the Comtesse de Bernonville, reading words that had brought to her mouth that dry, ironic, worldly smile?

Nina put out a hand, wanting to touch the miraculously painted fur of the cat. But in the same instant she felt a presence behind her in the gallery—and turned —and there was Dominique standing at some distance in a drift of light falling from a translucent inset in the ceiling.

"What do you think of her, Nina—my childhood self?" she asked in a voice scarcely above a murmur, but which came to Nina quite distinctly. "My young self, who had no way of knowing that pure happiness never lasts longer than a little?" Nina did not answer but stood staring at Dominique, and the cold terror of the courtyard, of that second in which she had seen

Domi's hand moving into her own, swept over her and she turned to the side and ran blindly—and stumbled into the leather-padded bench in the center of the room. She knelt there shaking but, curiously, with some small spark of an entirely different emotion from terror beginning to kindle inside of her. "Are you so frightened of me, then, Nina, now that you really know me? And yet because you refused to understand, I was forced to make you understand before I could tell you my story. I thought you had seen me for what I am, but when you came into the courtyard that evening after we ran over the grass, I realized that you still thought of me as no different from yourself, and so I did what I had to do. Have I been mistaken in depending on what I thought my father meant in my dream? You're not going to help us? I can't seem to know whether you are or not, and it means so much to me because I love my father. I think that by your world's measure there isn't very much time. Helena Staynes has finished her book on my father's life and she still doesn't know the truth of him. I've heard her say, though she has never wanted to believe it, that she is convinced he was a murderer."

Nina twisted round so that she was sitting on the bench and she was still shaking, and yet not now wholly with terror. Rather she was aware of a kind of bewildered excitement and she would never be able to explain how, between one instant and the next, this change had taken place. She had been chosen, by what means and for what reason she couldn't imagine, to give help in this inconceivable situation. In some queer way it had to do with Chagall's painting in the rotunda that both

[111]

she and Gil were drawn to—for quite different reasons
—and with Gil himself, who all unwittingly had directed
her here, where she would find Dominique, as Domi's
dream had foretold.

Now she heard voices in the room beyond, a man
questioning a guard, and his answer, and then a woman
laughing. She got up and took a step toward Domi.
"Auguste is in the courtyard," she said, "so we can't go
there. But I've seen a place, a kind of woody, ferny
place, opposite the little dining room—" Dominique
nodded, and Nina turned and went out of the gallery
just as the guard and the man and woman came in.

Chapter Thirteen

Domi was waiting for her. The path in the grotto
curved around from one entrance to another and in the
center of the curve was a pool and a rustic seat with
back and armrests contrived of twisted branches and
set in under the shadows of the overarching trees. From
it, one had a view of both entrances. Domi was at the
far end of the seat, her own Lisabetta clasped up to her,
and both were dappled over with moving shadows and
speckles of sunlight. Nina sat down at the near end of
the seat stiffly, shyly, as though meeting Dominique
for the first time, and she was shaken again by a kind
of involuntary shuddering so that she had to cross her
arms, her cold hands clutching her elbows, to try to
stop the shuddering by pressing her arms against herself.

"Don't be frightened of me, Nina." Domi's wide,
melancholy eyes asked it as much as her voice. "We
exist differently, perhaps, you and I, but we both exist.
We are both living beings, each in her own way, only
we can't touch one another, that's all."

"Yes—'What lies on the edge—'? It's only that we exist in different layers of time, isn't it, Domi?"

Domi nodded, her face brightening with relief. "There are worlds within worlds, each invisible to the other because we travel on different levels of awareness. Only rarely are some of us, for unexplained reasons, allowed to see beyond." Domi lifted Lisabetta and rubbed her cheek against the cat's fur as though she loved the feel of it and its fresh sweet scent.

"But, Domi, I should think that being dead—humanly dead, I mean, not spiritually—I should think you would know ahead. I should think you could *see* ahead. I've been thinking, and I still can't understand how it is that you need me."

Domi's eyes became larger than ever. "Know ahead!" she exclaimed. "Nina, if I could know ahead, I shouldn't be here. No, *p'tite*, I, like you, am still involved in a voyage of discovery. My self may no longer be encased in flesh and blood, but for me, too, the voyage continues."

They were quiet for a moment, and Nina could feel the spasmodic shaking begin to lessen, her whole body begin to relax. She twisted round now to face Domi, curling a leg under in her favorite listening position. "About your father," she said. "Tell me. I'm ready."

She had been born, Dominique began, when her mother Marie-Laure was seventeen. So that when Domi was eleven, Marie-Laure was twenty-eight and as full of delight in life as her daughter and as eager to get up early and go exploring through the morning fields, over the wooded hills, and around the edges of the lakes where the big rose-colored butoma blossoms stood above their own reflections. "Domi, Domi," Marie-Laure would call, bursting into Domi's bedroom at five-thirty of a spring morning. "I'm going out—do you want to come?" And Marthe, Domi's nurse, who had been Marie-Laure's only a breath in time before, so it seemed, rolled grumbling out of her soft bed to heat them milk over the fire. They'd catch their deaths in the damp grass, getting their feet sopping wet! And it wasn't seemly that a lady of breeding should take her child and go trolling around the countryside unattended. But they only laughed, while Domi scrambled into her clothes and presently, each with her basket for treasures, away they went down the dim staircase, across the enormous entrance hall whose arched ceiling was so high it was lost in shadow, and out the door with Lisabetta slipping after and then trotting on ahead to go mousing on her own.

All the plum trees on the hillsides circling the château were round clouds of white, and in the tilled valleys lines of vivid green were beginning to push up. But Domi and Marie-Laure were headed for the woods where the sparrows and chaffinches were working themselves into the mock battles of spring, doing their ritual dances and altogether behaving absurdly. Now the sun pierced the wood in long yellow lancets. Domi and Marie-Laure pressed back into damp hidden places to find gold and ivory and saffron mushrooms with their little hats of earth and mast tilted to one side. These went into their baskets, along with purple iris and violets, early foxgloves and pink-flowering horse chestnut. And when they got back to the château, Marie-Laure gave the cook the mushrooms to slice and brown in butter for breakfast while she herself put the flowers into bowls and vases and Domi ran up to ask Maurice, her father's valet, if her father was up yet. If, indeed, he was at the château at all and not off on another of "his dreary sieges in Paris," as Marie-Laure called them.

She went with him less and less, much as she loved him—this quiet, intense man whom she had married when she was sixteen. She wanted to be with him, yet the air of Paris stifled her. The atmosphere of intrigue and hatred and suppressed passions working at cross-purposes made her sick. She despised the women at court with their malicious gossiping and backbiting, their meaningless affairs and stupid pastimes. And so Kot, as she called her husband, came home as often as he could and for as long as he could, and after a while Domi understood that her father was beginning to abhor Napoleon as much as he had ever abhorred Louis XVI.

And now, when Domi was twelve, three things happened.

She remembers her father drinking his cognac after lunch and her mother sitting there with her own glass between her fingers and Domi was watching the sun sparkle in the stone of Marie-Laure's amethyst ring that Kot had given her when they were married. He was speaking of something he must do: he had to go to Napoleon.

"Now that he has conquered Italy, he is sacking Rome. He's stripping it of every painting of value, every statue, every monument. They may be ruined on the journey to France, but that is of no concern to him. He simply wants them, and that's the end of it. He told the Italians that the French army was coming 'to break their chains'! What a hypocrisy! And he promised them that their religion and their customs and their treasures would not be touched. That's what he said to them. And he lied. Perhaps, because I've been of service to him, he'll listen to me. How can we act like barbarians after all our talk of liberty, equality, and fraternity! For whom? For the French alone?"

A gray look came over Marie-Laure's face.

"But, Kot, you've already spoken out about so many things. You will be put into prison and I shall never see you again. God knows what will happen to you. And what good will it do? Napoleon will not pay the slightest attention—he will refuse to see you."

"But each one—each human being—must speak out. If a man believes something is wrong, immoral, he must speak. Otherwise he says 'Yes!' to the act of barbarism. If Napoleon won't see me, I will write him."

Napoleon would not see him and so Domi's father wrote the letter, and copies of it came to be circulated all over France. And the sack of Rome continued, and private villas and palaces and museums were looted of their treasures, and these were lost or pillaged or stolen. Libraries were torn apart and precious manuscripts destroyed for the gold ornaments of their bindings. The whole of Italy was plundered.

And that was the first thing that happened, the writing of Kot's letter, the first step on the downward path that led to the end.

In the next year, Marie-Laure died giving stillbirth to a second child. And after Marie-Laure's death, when

Domi's grandmother—Kot's mother—came to take charge, Domi and her father drew closer to each other than ever before. Now he confided to Domi his continually growing distrust of Napoleon as if she were not a child at all but a woman old enough to understand. And she did.

For the truth was that, underneath her lightheartedness, her joy in her own little world of engrossing countryside and the secure feeling that she was loved and protected and would be forever, she had always listened to her parents' conversation during mealtime. They had wanted her with them when they were alone and had never sent her away to eat with Marthe, so that everything that was happening in the outside world before Marie-Laure's death had been lying quiescent in her mind. Therefore she was ready to understand the second thing that happened: her father's horror over the kidnapping and shooting by Napoleon's soldiers of an old friend suspected, on the testimony of dubious witnesses, of being a party to a conspiracy to murder Napoleon.

"He was innocent, Domi. He had no real trial. And now I must speak up once again," and off he went to Paris. And when he came back he was closeted away for days at a time, writing, writing, always writing, or talking to Maurice, his valet, as if, instead of being simply a valet, Maurice was one of his closest confidants, as indeed he was—along with Jean Chrysostome—concerning affairs her father could not tell Domi for the sake of her own safety. Nor would he have dreamed of discussing these matters with his stern, stiff-necked old mother, who had always violently disapproved of her son's foolhardy outspokenness.

And then the third thing happened.

Napoleon proclaimed himself emperor. He had an imperial court and nobility. "And now," said Kot, "all those rights set down in our fine constitution, bought with so much blood, are shrinking to nothing."

"And are you going to speak out again, Papa?" Domi asked with a sense of cold fatality. She was thirteen, a young lady who dressed up and wore her mother's amethyst ring on those occasions when her father's guests came to the château and she was asked to play the harp or the harpsichord for them after dinner. She was quickly learning from her grandmother how to manage a great house in the country, for the old woman stayed stuffed up in her apartments and gave all orders for the running of the place through Domi. And Domi was learning too that the deep happiness and contentment she had known in those days when she had run free in the fields and woods with Marie-Laure, the days when her father had told her long tales of his boyhood, were gone. All that was over, and though she was still loved and protected, she lived with fear. At first she did not realize it, and then the knowledge began to impinge itself that no day went by without fear for her father.

In the end he was gone for almost three weeks without news of him reaching the château. At some time during the night of Friday of the second week, Domi woke and heard a sound outside her room, and somebody softly opened the door and stepped in.

"Papa?" she asked, her heart thudding. "Yes, it's just me, Domi," came a low voice. "I'm here now. Go to sleep." And she turned over with a sigh of relief and contentment and slept again. But when she woke the next morning and got up to go and greet him, she discovered Maurice, that gentle old man who had never done a living creature any harm in his whole life, lying near her father's untouched bed, murdered and covered with blood. And the sight of that vivid red soaked into his white nightrobe was something that stayed in her mind for the rest of her life as clearly and precisely as in the moment she first saw it.

She ran down the stairs screaming and calling. And uniformed, armed men came (but how quickly—as if they knew what had happened; as if they had been waiting!) and unaware of what she was doing, of what meaning her words could have, told them how she thought she had heard her father speak to her in the night, and had turned over and gone to sleep again.

"But where is he? Where is my father? Why isn't he here?"

And the men said that she was not to worry, that they would see that he was told. Then they wrapped up Maurice's body and took it away, and somebody cleaned up the blood near her father's bed.

The following week, one day in the late, gray, ice-cold afternoon, Domi and Marthe were sitting in front of the bedroom fire. Their feet were on footwarmers filled with hot poplar wood cinders covered with ashes. Marthe had pulled a nest of coals out of the fire and on these had put apples and chestnuts, and the fragrance of their roasting filled the air. Marthe was looking at an old mildewed book Kot had loved when he was a boy; it was worn to shreds and held in its pages the pressed petals of tulips and violets and the bearded impudent faces of spring pansies, which Domi had secreted there, all now translucent and delicate as the ghosts of flowers. And the breath of the turning pages crept out, an ancient, dried, musty scent that mingled with the smell of the apples and chestnuts. Domi had Lisabetta in her lap, her hand moving back and forth, stroking, stroking, while she listened to the silence of the winter afternoon, a silence broken only by the cawing of crows in the black woods and the moaning of wind around the casements. The muscles of Domi's stomach ached with waiting and her mind with trying to know what she was waiting for; her stomach had ached for days so that now she was dully used to the pain. And there was nothing to do but sit and listen for the sound of horses and carriage wheels.

But when the waiting came to an end, it came without the sound of her father's carriage. She heard shouting in the courtyard and the clatter of one horse's hooves, and she spilled Lisabetta from her lap and ran to the window. She looked down and saw a man, appearing squat and foreshortened—not her father—reining in his horse, and one of the menservants ran out and took a roll of paper from him and the horse with its rider turned and galloped away and Domi leaned her head against the window frame and could not move.

Presently her grandmother came in and stood by the door, waiting in silence until Domi should turn and face her. "Dominique," she said, "your father has been accused of conspiring against the Emperor and of murdering Maurice because the old man knew too much of what your father was involved in. Your father was tried yesterday morning, and when he would say nothing, would not tell where he has been during these past weeks nor what he has been doing, he was court-martialed and shot."

After her grandmother closed the door, the dusk drew in and Domi still stood rigid at the window, while Marthe wept by the fire. And when it grew dark, one of the servingmen came and lit the candles and put more logs on and took out the apples and chestnuts from the coals. Then food was brought on a tray, but neither Domi nor Marthe touched it. After a while Domi, without taking off her clothes, crept into bed and lay there feeling nothing. But presently she learned for the first time that she could not cry as other children cry. Her crying was an agonizing, heaving convulsion that so distorted her face that later Marthe said she scarcely recognized her. Her ribs felt as if they had been beaten.

In the early hours of the morning, because she could not sleep, she got up and went to the window and saw the frozen countryside shimmering under the moonlight, the hills and dark woods laid over with silver and the river glittering between its silver banks. In a tree below her window a little sparrow owl imitated a cat, and Lisabetta answered. Domi stood there watching and listening, then turned back to her bed and fell asleep. And in that exhausted, haunted state, she dreamed the dream of finding herself in a huge building that was not her home, in which the furniture of the château was set about in unfamiliar patterns and the houses beyond the windows were not clusters of little red-roofed cottages down in the valley, but tall, narrow buildings pressed up against one another directly facing her over there on the other side of lawns and flower beds and a high stone wall and iron gates. Through the iron gates she saw ugly carriages going by, low and rounded and shiny and hard that, terrifyingly, seemed to move all of themselves and at times let out harsh cries.

Then somehow she was in her own bedroom (but how bare it was!) and there was a hall outside the door, a hall with glowing cases which were set into the wall, and in the cases were all sorts of objects on shelves, some the possessions of her own family and others she had never seen before. She was crouched up in the corner of her bed with Lisabetta by her when a girl in a short dress came and stood in the doorway, and then her father was standing there behind the girl and saying without words that she would help them. The girl stared at Dominique and after a moment turned and ran off and Dominique scrambled from the bed and went toward her father saying, "I will never rest until I've proved you innocent—I swear it—I swear it!" and her father gave her a long, steady, loving look and smiled, and that was all. He was no longer there and Domi woke from her dream knowing that she had not seen him and would never see him. But the dream had been as clear and detailed and immediate as anything that had ever happened to her in real life.

Domi was still holding Lisabetta. And just as she had on that late, ice-cold winter afternoon in the château when she had been sitting in front of the fire with

Marthe, waiting for news of her father, she stroked and stroked Lisabetta the whole time she had told Nina her story. Nina, while Domi was speaking, had lived inside that other time, seeing each scene as Domi described it, herself *being* that far-off Dominique. So that now, with Domi silent and the story ended, she looked away and felt herself, almost as much as Domi must, a stranger in this world of the present century.

"And your father, Domi—you never proved him innocent?"

"But if I had—don't you understand, Nina?—my dream about you would have meant nothing. I would never have had it. All my life, in this world, I searched for the facts of what happened to my father in those last weeks before he was shot. Where had he been? Why would he never tell where he had been? I was always certain Maurice had known but I never found out a single thing. It was as if my father had stepped off the edge of the earth. Forever after, in all the historical records, which the whole world has read and believes are true, my father has been a traitor who was once called the conscience of Napoleon, and the murderer of an innocent old man who loved him all his life and whom my father loved in return. He would no more have harmed Maurice than he would have harmed me or my mother or his own mother. And he was never a traitor, but he had the courage to speak out about what he felt to be wrong, and there is a vast difference. He would never have conspired to murder Napoleon because he felt that to murder someone you disagree with is barbarism, and that it does no good in the long run because such an evil only begets further evil."

"But, Domi—it was all so long ago! If somehow I can help you to prove him innocent, what good will it do *him*?"

"It will do *a* good. It will set straight one more lie. As for time, that is nothing. Two hundred years—what are they? But truth is something, and Mrs. Staynes is writing a lie. You remember I told you that she is doing a book of my father's life, which is why she went to the château in the first place and then found she could buy pieces of our furniture and the paneling and some of the fireplaces for the museum. You are a friend of hers."

"In a way—almost."

"Sometime, perhaps, you could talk to her about her work. She has sent off her manuscript to the publisher, this much I know. But she must have a copy; it would be absurd not to have. Perhaps you could ask to see it, Nina, a copy of her book, because even though she is finished I can tell that she is still baffled and dissatisfied."

Lisabetta slipped from under Domi's hands, looked into Nina's eyes, and Nina instinctively reached to pick her up. But Lisabetta drifted through her fingers, and Nina shivered and looked up through the trees and saw that the sky had turned gray.

"You must go, Nina," said Dominique. "See, the museum is closing. The people are coming out and Auguste will be locking the gates."

Nina went to the entrance of the grotto and saw Gil

on the steps of the museum. "Nina!" He waved and began walking over and she turned and went back under the trees toward the bench, but Dominique was gone. When Gil arrived he looked around as if puzzled. "Who've you been talking to? Was someone here?"

Nina was sitting on the arm of the branch seat and she was smiling because of Lisabetta. "What do you mean? There isn't anyone—as you can see." No, but Lisabetta—Domi's Lisabetta—was sitting right behind him busily washing her left leg which was stuck straight out in front of her, and now she spread her toes and got to work on them with a strong pink tongue.

"It seemed as if—" He frowned. "I don't know. It was a funny feeling I had. Anyhow, Mam'zelle was asking about you, and when I said I'd seen you coming up the hill ahead of me, she wanted me to find you because she has something to tell you."

Nina remembered the evening Mam'zelle had taken her home. "What, Gil? What do you think? Didn't she say?"

"I think it has something to do with vacation."

"So do I. When she took me home one night— the night I passed out in the courtyard—she said that I might change in the next few weeks, let alone before summer vacation. And after a bit I knew what she was thinking: that I could come and work."

Chapter Fourteen

On Saturday morning, Nina came through Mam'zelle's outer office and crossed the rotunda to confide to Mr. Quarles her incredible news. They were actually going to pay her (a possibility that hadn't, for some reason, entered her head) to do what she would have chosen to do this summer above all else. It wouldn't be very much, Mam'zelle had said, because Nina was untrained: she would come principally to learn. Still, she might earn as much as thirty or forty dollars during the summer. It would all depend. She would start by putting a pile of costume plates back in their proper places and do some filing in the registrar's office—if she could file accurately. In this way, Mam'zelle said, Nina could begin absorbing what went on behind the scenes. Mr. Quarles was satisfyingly impressed but by the gleam in his eye he might have known what Mrs. Henry intended.

"Mother and Dad don't understand," Nina told him, "why Mam'zelle has chosen me—at my age."

"You may tell them," said Mr. Quarles in his precise,

old-fashioned way, "that it is really very simple. She likes you. She's interested in you."

In Mam'zelle's office, "Who knows, Nina," she had said, "but that someday you may be sitting in this chair of mine, in the years to come."

"I know," said Nina. "I've thought of that—and I'm going to be."

"Such assurance!" exclaimed Mam'zelle. "I had nothing like it at your age, about anything important. However, perhaps you should know that when I retire in a few years, Helena Staynes will be taking my place."

"Yes, but then," Nina said, turning to Mrs. Staynes, "couldn't I be the registrar and in charge of costumes?"

"I haven't a doubt of it, Nina," Helena Staynes said. "I haven't a doubt. And if not in this museum, then perhaps in some other."

"Oh, no, *this* one," said Nina. "*This* one."

It wasn't, oddly enough, until she went over to stand in front of *Time Is a River Without Banks* that she thought of Domi. However, Dominique was nowhere to be found. She was not in any of the château rooms, nor in the grotto across the lawn, or in any of the galleries where the paintings were. Nina went upstairs, where she had never been, and wandered disconsolately among the prints and etchings, the cases of silver and jewelry and chinaware, and an exhibit of the clothing the men and women of France had once arrayed themselves in. Finally she went back to the grotto, but it was filled with the feeling of absence.

There was nothing to do, then, but the deadly dull shopping for the weekend for which she'd been given a list. She was to be home in time for lunch at one, after which she and her parents had been invited for the late afternoon and for dinner by some new friends of Mrs. Harmsworth's living out beyond Golden Gate Park. Tedious, it would be, and the conversation boring, all about politics and the state of the world and people Nina didn't know. She would take Odile's journal and some writing paper so that she could write a letter to Maizie Hudson and ask about Windy, and to Mrs. Bourne to tell her about her summer job at the museum.

She was about to leave the grotto when two women wandered by as though thoroughly enjoying the sun and air and each other's company. Their arms were linked and they kept looking around as they talked, and up at the sky from which a sea wind was sweeping the last puffs of fog. "No," said the stout one, "it would never do—not for us. There was no place for Joan, only a sort of cubbyhole. And the bedroom was far too small. A pity, considering the view—"

Nina stood concentrating while they strolled on, reached the gate, and disappeared. Then she tore after them, and when she caught up, lightly touched the arm of the stout one, who turned, startled. Was it for rent, Nina asked, the place with the view?

"Why, yes, it is. Up on the fourth floor at the top of a house over on Museum Street, the one that ends just beyond the museum and runs into this one. Here—" and the stout woman began digging into her purse. "A real estate agent gave me the address."

"A little place," said Nina, "but with a cubbyhole for me—"

"Space enough for a bed and that's about it, and a closet for a kitchen," said the woman, rooting amongst oddments.

"But we could turn in a circle and get dinner in two minutes—"

"And there's a mingy bathroom—no bathtub—"

"But a shower would be enough—and there's a view—"

"Oh, yes, views and views, if that helps any." The woman was still vigorously rooting.

"Like a tree house—"

"A tree house badly in need of redoing. There's a sort of fireplace, but it smokes to judge by the wallpaper. Where could the confounded thing have got to—that's my shopping list. It was on a *card*—"

"A *fireplace*?"

"Yes, but of course wood is expensive, and then the whole apartment is extremely small and shabby—"

"But we could paint it! *I* could paint it! I *can* paint!"

"Ah, here it is—I knew I hadn't thrown it away. See, now, two blocks over and one block up, and there's the rent that's being asked, and the telephone number in case the landlady isn't at home."

"But of course I'd just sit and wait—"

"Yes, well, don't get your hopes up, dear. I was there yesterday and it's probably taken by now."

All the tall old houses opposite the museum were from the early 1900s, elaborate in the extreme, with scrollwork, scalloped clapboarding on the upper stories, carved insets, the front windows all bays—the very sign and symbol of San Francisco housefronts—square bays, oblong bays, slanted bays, curved bays, and the corners of roofs topped by gables, witches'-hat turrets, and cupolas. Most had apparently been painted within the last two or three years, some white, some gray or dark green with white trim, and there were small flourishing gardens behind the brickwork at the front along the sidewalk and below the iron scrolls of the railings going up the steep front steps. They continued the two blocks across from the museum grounds and around the corner onto Museum Street. Because little California towns like Silverspring, dating from the early days of settlement, all have their Victorian and Edwardian houses, for Nina they were a part of her life. As she glanced up at the house number she had already memorized, and started up the steps, the excrescences and scrollwork looked to her like home.

She rang, saw that the door was ajar with a bag of groceries sitting inside, rang again, and when she got no answer, cogitated. You went right into apartment houses, but was this an apartment building or a flat? She picked up the bag and stepped into the entry hall, finding herself at the open door of a room in which a little squat woman, on the far side of it, was gazing fixedly at herself in a tall, antique mirror with a heavy gilt frame hanging above the marble-topped table against which she leaned. The room itself was shadowy, large and—Nina took in by osmosis—fascinating. It wasn't particularly Victorian in its furnishings, only crowded, and Nina had the impression that you would never be at a loss for things to do or to look at or to imagine in that room. The walls were covered with paintings, the tables were full of objects. The heavy draperies, two or three screens, and two long couches all added to an effect rich, cluttered, and inviting.

Nina stood motionless, the bag of groceries in her arms. She could see a part of herself in the mirror over the shoulder of the woman, who continued to stare at her own face with bruised-looking eyes and an expression of intense longing. Then she apparently became aware of Nina, and gave a cry and turned.

"Oh," she said in a tone of deep disappointment, "you're real."

"Yes," said Nina, "I am. I'm terribly sorry." It was the only possible reply to a statement full of such poignant regret.

The little woman, not fat but waistless like a bolster, and with a lined, rather striking ivory face and worn mouth, came toward her. "I can imagine what you're thinking." She tapped her own head. "But, you see, I've always had an odd feeling about mirrors—"

Nina had put the groceries on a chair inside the door, never once taking her eyes from the woman's face. "You *have*? But so have I! Only I've never said anything. And I've wondered—"

"What did you wonder?"

"Well, if a person could ever catch everything off guard behind him, if a person might see something—or *some*one he'd never catch sight of in the everyday world."

"I know. I've had an idea ever since my accident. I keep thinking about it off and on—the idea, I mean— and I felt, just as I unlocked the door, that I must try it: not just glance in the mirror to see if my hair's straight or I need lipstick, but have the courage to really look, to steadily look, press my way in." The tired eyes searched Nina's, then she sighed. "Ah, well, it's been so long since I was like you—"

She stopped, and there were voices in the street outside and then a car door slammed. Suddenly Nina tore open her purse, got out her wallet, unfolded the ten dollar bill her mother had given her for the shopping, and pushed it into the hand of the squat little woman. "I've rented the apartment. I've *rented* it and *no*body can take it. Oh, *please* don't let anybody take it!" The little woman's mouth fell open in astonishment. "It's all the money I've got right now, but as long as I'm here first, surely you wouldn't let some grownup—"

"But, honey," the little woman said, "you haven't seen it. And your parents haven't. What will they say?"

"But we can't *stand* where we are now! We hate it —we loathe it! And I don't care if the rooms up in your apartment *are* shabby and need painting. I don't care about anything but the view and the air and the light, and my mother and dad won't either. Oh, please—" The voices continued outside, as though in some final discussion. "Please keep the money."

All at once the little woman smiled at Nina; her eyes shone, her whole face changed. "Oh, I remember!" she said. "I remember wanting things so desperately at your age. Here, take the key and run on up."

Nina thudded up three flights without stopping once, shakingly fitted the key into the lock—and walked in.

A bird's nest. A tree house. An eagle's eyrie. Sun poured, flooded into the long bare living room where silence brooded until a single fly buzzed somewhere. There was a strong smell of fireplace. Nina went to each tall window in turn, all around, furnishing the rooms with the family furniture and looking down and away over varying views in a state of uplifted tranquillity. This was all theirs now: the tracery of diminishing, threadlike streets; the turreted or gabled or flat housetops, some of the flat ones hidden in little roof gardens; the wooded hills of Marin County standing up away to the northwest on this windswept, smogless day and, closer, a traffic of tugs and barges, fishing boats, little sailboats and freighters going about their business on waters moving out into the Golden Gate. Over there to the east she saw three islands sitting in the bay, and a bridge stretching over to the minute cities of Berkeley and Oakland with their summer hills behind them.

She found her cubbyhole with space for a single twin bed and perhaps a chest of drawers and a chair. The bathroom was assuredly mingy and the kitchen just big enough to turn in. "Convenient," Nina remarked aloud. "And, Mother," she said, going back into the living room, "let's have our dining table here, at this end, where we can look out over the city and see the fire in the fireplace at the same time." Then she was still suddenly, her hands gripped together. "Mother—Dad! I've found it. *I've found our place—our own, right place.*"

A minute or so later she was rattling downstairs and heard the landlady's voice in the hall and a young couple arguing. Nina swung round the corner above the ground floor and hung there, poised, her hand on the banister and one foot in space. "—this morning! I *told* you this morning we'd be back," the girl was saying in a loud voice as if the little squat woman were deaf. "I *told* you we had to measure our furniture before we could be absolutely sure, and I *told* you we'd lease it. It's perfect—exactly what we want. Here's our check for the full amount, first month and last—" The girl glanced up and took in Nina. "Is that the one you were talking about?"

"It is," said the little woman. "And I've already told you she's given me her money. She beat you to it —that's the size of the matter. Now, if you—"

"But you can't rent an apartment to a kid!" shouted the young man in a fury. "It's not legally binding and her parents haven't even—"

"That's right. And if they don't want it, I may let you know. Right this minute I'd like my lunch, so I'll have to ask you to leave—" With surprising force she backed them out of the door, shut it, and turned and smiled up at Nina with a wry, dry smile. "I'll tell you something. They'd be the last people on earth I'd let know about anything. For one thing, women who talk at me as if I'm stupid or can't understand the language, and men who try to mow me down by shouting at me, make me curl. For another, I've known all kinds of renters and those two would never let up for a day wanting things done." She held out her hand as Nina came down to her with the key. "My name's Edna Kendrick. What's yours?"

On some other occasion she had come into this food-and dust-smelling apartment, closed the door and leaned

[135]

against it without saying anything. Yes, on that night, weeks ago, when she'd got lost in the rain coming home from the museum for the first time. But that had been a silence of wretchedness and revulsion.

"Nina?" Mrs. Harmsworth came in drying her hands on a kitchen towel. "It's a quarter past one, dear, and I thought—why, where are the groceries? Didn't you shop?"

"Mother." Nina went to her and put her arms around her. "Mother, I didn't buy any groceries because I didn't have any money."

"But I gave you ten dollars!"

"I know. And it isn't lost. I spent it. I gave it to Mrs. Edna Kendrick so that she'll hold an apartment until we can all go and see it together. Oh, Mother— Dad—" and she looked beyond to her father, who had come along the hall from the bedroom, "I have our own place. I *have* it. Will you come and see? Couldn't we go now? Oh, if only I could make you know how beautiful it is—"

"*Beau*tiful!" Her mother stared at Nina as if she were mad—stark mad not to realize that the last thing on earth the Christopher Harmsworths could afford was something beautiful, anything beautiful. "Nina, how *could* you have done this when it only means we've lost ten dollars. How much is the rent? *Why* wouldn't you even—"

"But, Mother, Mother—listen to me. Dad, listen. It's high up, and we can have air, and light, and we can see all over, clear to the ends of the earth. And there's a little fireplace, even, and a little, small room for me, and the rent's only fifteen dollars more a month than here. Think of it! It needs painting, but Mrs. Kenrick'll take off five dollars a month because I'm going to do it—"

"*You're* going to do it! But we can't even afford ten dollars more a month, let alone the expense of moving and getting the furniture down from Silverspring! I think that woman must be out of her mind to let a child do this without phoning, without asking—"

"Oh, no, Mother, she's not out of her mind. She's just like me. We understand each other. Why, when I went in she was looking into a mirror and she feels about mirrors the way I do. And she says she remembers exactly how it feels to be my age, to want something more than you can bear, like me wanting to get us out of here. And she took the money and trusted me, and never even once said anything about my being a kid. And, Mother and Dad, I have a job. In the museum. And I may earn as much as forty dollars—"

"You mean a *month*?"

"Oh, no—altogether. Though maybe they'd keep me on—for the whole vacation, I mean—to work now and then if I'm good at things." There was a short, tense silence in which Mr. Harmsworth turned to the window and stood there looking out with his hands in his back pockets. "Dad?" Nina cried, going to him and putting her hands on his arm, "Dad, don't you want to get out of here? Aren't you glad I've found something?" He did not answer and she could not read the expression on his face, though in an anguish of bewilderment she tried to turn him so that she could look into his eyes.

[137]

Somehow, she felt in a flash of perception, what was going through his mind went deeper than a mere change of rooms.

"You're determined to stay, Nan?" he asked. "I mean in this city?"

"Why, of course we're going to stay!" exclaimed Mrs. Harmsworth. "Chris, I don't know what you—"

"Don't you?" Then he turned his head and looked at Nina, and there was that little almost-smile just quivering at the corners of his eyes, at the corners of his mouth. "You want that other apartment with your whole soul, don't you, Squirrel? Perhaps, Nan—perhaps tomorrow we could at least go and look at what Nina's found. And if you lose the ten dollars because it isn't right, she can pay you back—"

"Oh, it *isn't* just that, Chris—it isn't just *that*—"

"No. But let's go and look anyway."

Chapter Fifteen

Mrs. Kendrick was sitting on a box in the sunlight that had been coming and going all day long while Nina blissfully spread sun-colored paint onto the living room walls with a roller. Etruscan Gold, it said on the paint can. Nina was doing all the walls because that was easy, and her father would do the enamel on the doors and woodwork.

Mrs. Kendrick was telling her what she had been searching for in the mirror that day they had first met. It had been her other self, her real self, her young self. "Sometimes it seems as if I've always been like this," she said, "misshapen, unattractive—"

Oh, no! Not unattractive, Nina wanted to reassure her, not even now. And she wanted to tell Mrs. Kendrick that she must once have been very beautiful, only you can't say a thing like that to a woman: must once have been.

"—and yet at other times, when I can almost forget my hurts and the way I look, I think it can't be that

that girl is really lost forever, buried and never recognized by anyone, but still there. Oh, yes, she is, Nina—as young as you, my dear." Mrs. Kendrick was silent for a little while Nina painted, and then, "I've brought up the book I told you about this morning, the one my sister gave me in the hospital, the one that has the part about the mirror in it, about searching. I thought of you especially because of your friend who is so interested in time. Listen! 'The mirror has always delighted me because whatever it reflects seems to sink down through layers and layers of time as through water, so that one's own face becomes someone else's face long ago, and the flowers I set there, especially the peonies and shirley poppies, take on a magic solubility in the reflection as if they were floating away through time, as indeed they are—' "

Paint was sliding down Nina's arm and she absentmindedly wiped it off with an old torn undershirt of her father's. She was standing at the top of a stepladder doing high up under the molding, the last patch that would finish the living room; and she would look around every now and then, unable to believe that she, Nina Harmsworth, all by herself, had accomplished this remarkable transformation. She had even done the ceiling. "And have you found your other face yet, Mrs. Kendrick? Your other self—your young self?"

"No, dear, not yet. But then it takes courage to go on looking with all the desire and strength a person has. Maybe more than I can manage. And maybe the past just isn't there. And yet—listen to this. 'Katrine has died since I came here, so she is one of the presences who come and go at this strange intersection where I do not live in time, but where past and future flow together into the present as gently as the currents of air that sometimes make the curtains stir as if a hand just touched them.' You see, Nina, someone else feels what I feel. Perhaps I'm thinking I can get to that strange intersection—there in the mirror."

Nina laid the roller in the paint pan and looked down at Mrs. Kendrick intently. " 'One of the presences at this strange intersection where I do not live in time.' That means our time, the way we think about it. And that's what Domi is: a presence at a strange intersection. I must tell her. She'll like that."

"And who is Domi?"

"A friend of mine at the museum. Someone I'm trying to help."

"And why is she a presence at a strange intersection? Is she like Katrine?"

"In a way, and yet not. We both exist, she says, only on different levels."

"Yes, that has occurred to me. Pain's led me into a territory of thinking I've never ventured on before: that there could be different levels of awareness, of existence. Though of course I realize it's perfectly possible there's nothing at the end but darkness and silence and nonbeing. Yet, here is your Domi. Someday tell me about her and whether you were able to help."

Nina reflected for a little, still looking at Mrs. Kendrick. Then she got down from the ladder to go and wash her hands and arms. "I have to see her. I have a feeling she'll be there, at the museum. All at once, right now, I have this feeling, and there's something I've been thinking about that she's got to know."

What had come to Nina was that perhaps Domi needed to read those entries in the second volume of Odile's journal having to do with the man, whose initial was K, whom Odile wrote of again and again, even in his absence. This second volume, in French, that Helena Staynes had spoken of, could be one that she owned, or it might be Mam'zelle's and kept in her office.

Nina waited now in front of Mr. Quarles's desk while he answered the questions of two boys who had come in ahead of her. Looking beyond him she saw Dominique at the entrance of a gallery opening off the rotunda opposite to that of the château rooms on the other side. She was standing there in her sea-green dress, quite still, with an expression of grave anticipation on her face, her eyes fixed upon Nina. Nina pointed to herself, then toward Mam'zelle's office, then indicated to Dominique that she would meet her in the grotto. Dominique nodded as if—yes, she expected as much.

Later, when Nina came to the grotto with volume two of Odile's journal in her hand, Dominique was waiting. Silently Nina held it out so that Dominique could see the title and then sat down beside her. "Domi," she said, "have you ever heard Mam'zelle or anyone mention that Odile Chrysostome kept a journal? No? Well, you wouldn't have read it in your time because it was only discovered and published about fifteen years ago. Mam'zelle happened to have volume one in English and she has given it to me and I've read it twice, almost three times. Just now Mr. Quarles found volume two in French for me in Mam'zelle's office and he's let me borrow it. Domi, I'm excited. I think I've thought of something. What did you say Marie-Laure called your father?"

"Kot. She always called him that, and so did Grandmother."

"Did anyone else?"

Domi paused. "I don't remember that anyone—no, it was a very private family name. I know that none of my father's political friends who came to the château ever called him that, only Antoine if they knew him well. His name was Clovis Antoine de Lombre" (Clovee An-twan, Nina echoed in her own mind) "and perhaps he couldn't say Clovis when he was little and somehow made Kot out of it."

"And was it always spelled with a K, or with a C?"

"With a K. Odd, I suppose, as Clovis begins with a C, and yet he always signed his letters to Mama Kot with a K."

"Domi, did Chrysostome, Odile's father, call him Kot?"

"Yes—yes, he did. I think he was the only one outside of the family who called him that. Surely Odile doesn't speak of my father as Kot!"

"No. She speaks of someone she puts down as K. Just that initial. And this person she writes about as K she loved very much. I mean, I think that she must have been in love with him. I don't know why she didn't realize it."

"Odile in love with my *father*? But that's preposterous! She couldn't have meant Kot. She was a child—nothing but a child!"

"Oh, no. In the beginning, when she first wrote the

journal, she was fifteen, and that's not exactly a child. But she didn't seem to know then *how* she loved him. She thought she cared about him as a special friend, maybe the way her father did, and she resented it when her family teased her. She said they didn't understand, that after all she knew K was married—she kept that in mind. But if she didn't love him in a special way, you see, she wouldn't have *had* to keep it in mind. And when he came to visit, she was filled with almost more than happiness. I remember her saying, 'K is coming, and there are no words shining enough to put beside those three.' When your mother died—or at least when K's wife died—Odile put 'K has no wife now. He has come to us and he is very sad.' But never once did she put down the name of K's wife, or if he had any children. And I thought that was very interesting. It was as if—all the way through—she didn't want K to have any family life outside of the one he had in her own family."

"*Sad!*" repeated Dominique incredulously. "*Sad!* Why, he worshiped my mother—he was heartbroken."

"Domi, listen! Odile goes on writing about K in volume two. I know because I flipped through as soon as Mr. Quarles handed it to me. I couldn't wait. So I'll hold the book and turn the pages while you hunt for wherever it tells about K, because I've been thinking that maybe, as they were so close, he told Odile something, or the family, that could help us discover what happened to him."

"Nina—is the week of December 10, 1804, scattered with the initial K?"

Nina turned over the pages, turned and turned,

until she had reached the last pages of the book. "Yes, and a few days before. All scattered with K. December 14th is the last entry, but there is nothing between December 10th and the 14th. Why do you ask?"

"Because," said Domi, "December 10, 1804, was the day my father was shot. What does she say at the end? Let me see. Hold the book. '*Nous avons les nouvelles. Papa désire que j'épouse Carondel. Ce ne fait rien. Ma vie est finie. Je ne peux plus écrire.*'" Domi was silent for a moment. "Yes, Nina, you are right. K *is* Kot. It was my father Odile loved—it was my father who was at the Chrysostomes the last week of his life and on the night Maurice was murdered at the château. She says, 'We have the news. Papa wants me to marry Carondel. It doesn't matter. My life is finished. I can write no more.' And now, Nina, hold the book so that I can read back over those days before he left the Chrysostomes. Turn back for a week or so. There—December 3rd he comes to them. Now turn ahead, further, further. Yes, he is with them the whole time until almost the end, in secret. And not one of them would tell me that—not one. Not more than a year after my father's death I went to them. By then Chrysostome himself was dead and Odile had married Carondel. I never saw her—they had moved away and most of the Chrysostome family were scattered. But I asked Madame Chrysostome and Gabrielle and Cyprian if they could tell me anything— anything at all—and they would say nothing. And the whole time I was talking to them they knew that my father had been there, all during those last days before he finally went to Paris and was shot for a murder he couldn't possibly have committed because he was over

[145]

a hundred miles away from where Maurice and Grandmother and I were waiting for him. Witnesses accused him of being seen on certain days and at certain places in Paris, meeting with known subversives, places he could not possibly have been because of those days he was in Pontoise. Now, I shall read, Nina, and I'll translate as I go."

And so Nina held open the book and Domi leaned close, always closer in her absorption, until Nina looked down and saw Domi's form merged with her own, could scarcely tell which was sea-green silk and which her own gray skirt, which was her arm and which was Domi's, the two lying in their laps together, one within the other, under the moving shadows of the leaves or in spots of sunlight. Coldness crept through her, the inexplicable coldness of the courtyard, but she did not move, only sat quiet and listened to Domi's voice reading softly in her ear.

3 DECEMBER 1804

"When I woke this morning, I said aloud, the moment I opened my eyes, 'K is under this roof!' I heard him arrive very early when it was still dark. There came the sound of hooves along the lane that leads from the main road across the fields to our farm buried in its trees and gardens. I got up and looked out, and all around, the countryside lay softly alight in its blanket of snow—no moon, only the close-set stars. And long before the horseman drew up and I heard him light from his horse then rap on the door, *I knew.* How could I not know! 'It's K!' and I snatched up my robe, washed my face in water that only a moment before had had a thin skin of ice over it in the pitcher, and brushed out my hair. But just as I was about to step into the hall I heard Mama go swiftly by, and then heard Papa downstairs quietly unbolt the door and heard their voices, K's and Mama's and Papa's mingled in greeting. And I heard K ask Papa if he could stay with us in complete privacy until he must leave again next week. Because of conditions in Paris, where Napoleon has just crowned himself emperor and all who were once close to him but now have the audacity to criticize are suspect, K wants no one to know where he is. He left Paris late yesterday afternoon, coming through woods and over the hills so as not to be seen. As Papa said, there is no reason in the world why anyone should be aware he is here. We are quite self-sufficient. The boys do the field and garden work and no housemaids are needed with Mama and three girls to do the cooking and cleaning, which is fortunate considering the little Papa makes from his paintings. Yes, we shall keep K to ourselves as we usually do, and none shall know of him so long as he cares to stay.

"K has come, he says, because he has such a great need to talk to Papa. They went off at once to have a glass of brandy, and Mama hurried to make coffee and get K something to eat. Then I heard Cyprian go down to take care of K's horse. Meanwhile, I stood there in my new robe that I have just finished, my face washed and my hair brushed, unable to move and yet wanting with every pulse of my blood to go down and join that warm murmur of voices in front of the fire that I knew was burning in the kitchen. I heard Lubo, who loves K as much as if he were K's own dog, giving little yelps and whines of excitement when he was let in from the scullery. But I—no, *I* could not go down. Not yet, knowing what I now know about myself, certain that were I to enter the kitchen with everyone sitting there, looking round to greet me, K getting up and coming over, I would be quite unable to keep my knowledge from shining in my face for everyone to see. I should have to arrange differently, give that look to K alone in some secret moment to be managed just how, I hadn't planned.

"It was at the end of this past summer that the truth of my feelings came to me. K and I had gone out into the countryside together in the *petit-duc*, the two-seated carriage with no coachman's box, which I always choose when K says he would like to go for a little drive. 'Zandre, in his silver-buckled harness, browsed by the wayside as he drew us slowly along, and because the cart's body is set so low, I could hop off and gather oak apples and wild strawberries and hedge roses without interrupting 'Zandre's dreamy progress through the sunlit country. Swallowtails and white admirals and purple emperors were hovering over the fields and wayside ditches, and K told me another story of his boyhood when he went with his parents to Spain and Germany and the Netherlands and even as far away as Russia. But presently he fell silent and his silence gradually closed over me until I put my arm through his and laid my face against him.

" 'What is it, K?' I asked. 'What is it? Why are you so quiet? Tell me.'

"Because he reached up and covered my hand with his own and turned his face and I felt his cheek pressed against my forehead and then felt him draw away suddenly as though reminding his emotions that they had forgotten themselves, I knew for the first time in what way I loved him. Not as a daughter or a niece or as a family friend, but as a woman loves a man she wants to spend the rest of her life with. We said little for the remainder of the journey and K left for home that evening.

"All during lunch today my father and K talked, and all during the afternoon, sometimes in the studio, sometimes in the little walled garden, walking, walking back and forth, as though they could never be finished. And when I might pass near, K would look at me, say nothing, only meet my eyes. And tonight after supper I could bear it no longer, and took a lantern and went to the barn saying I wanted to see if Louette, our white cat, who has just borne another litter, was taking care of her kittens in their straw-filled box: Louette, one of the most practiced and watchful of mothers, having brought up at least four families! I ran across the snow in the quiet darkness, and the frosty air bit my nostrils. In the warm, clean, animal-smelling barn, I hung my lantern on a nail and slipped between the Friesians, those placid creatures who look so beautiful by lantern-light. And no sooner had they swung their heads round to greet me than the door of the barn opened again and K stood there—and held out his arms—and I went to him.

"I will not confide even here the moments that followed. They belong to K and me alone and shall stay with me in silence for the rest of my life, to be recalled only with him. Sufficient to say that we are promised to one another and have told Papa and Mama and the family, who are all astonished out of their wits—not at the revelation of my love for K, but of his for me. Yes, as far as they are concerned, I shall always be nothing but "the little one." Papa says he will never forget the expressions on our faces as we came into the house together, and he immediately commanded us to stand just there, in the doorway, as we were, so that he could make a sketch. And he did make a sketch, and captured that instant forever."

4 DECEMBER 1804

"*Mon Dieu!* Today Carondel, our neighbor, came over in his best black suit, and Mama, seeing him get out of his carriage, shooed K into the studio where Papa is getting on with the painting he is making from the sketch. What do you suppose Carondel had come for, arrayed in his Sunday suit? Why, to ask for my hand! It isn't to be believed. Here are Gabrielle and Simone, older, more dignified, more attractive in every way, both able to sew, to cook to perfection, to keep the house in admirable condition, in fact both highly accomplished in all the arts of housewifery—and he wants me! Of course this was not known at first. Carondel asked very courteously to speak to Papa, and Papa was called and took Carondel into the parlor, where they had a short conversation. Papa is a wicked mischief. He insisted upon having me in, just in order, he confessed afterwards, to be able to behold the expression on my face and to hear how I would handle this absurd situation. I am ashamed, but it was all I could do to keep from bursting out laughing. Carondel, that good, kind, serious farmer, earnest, capable, quite wealthy (I might add!), sat there looking at me as if my single word would give him life or death. And I had to tell him that under no circumstances could I be thought to have any notion whatsoever of marrying anyone—*right now*. And Papa said that as I was the one concerned, my word was final. But could not a marriage be arranged for the future, as long as no one else was being considered for my hand, Carondel wanted to know in enormous surprise, obviously astounded at his reception, as he is in all ways so very desirable. No, no, I replied, getting up in confusion, fighting with myself not to laugh and knowing my face was turning scarlet, and would he forgive me if I asked to be excused? I made my escape and went running off to the studio where K and Mama and the girls were waiting for me, flung my arms around K's waist and got my crazy laughter over with, then told them what had happened, finishing up with, 'Imagine that poor old man of *forty*!' Whereupon K reminded me with the strangest expression that he himself was thirty-five. To this I replied, with the unerring logic of my kind, that I wouldn't have cared if he were ninety!"

8 DECEMBER 1804

"Papa has almost finished our painting, and the entire family has pronounced it his masterpiece, the finest likeness he has ever made of K and certainly the best he has ever done of me. Happiness, he told us, might very well have had something to do with its success, as his best work seems always to come out of either great joy, or pain, but rarely out of anything in

[151]

between. Of course he did not mean physical pain, Papa being an extraordinarily healthy and energetic man. No, he meant, I knew, out of search and struggle. The harder the bite of life on either side of the balance, the more powerful the work."

"K will leave tonight and will be back in Paris tomorrow morning. I couldn't bear to let him go if I did not know that he will be away only long enough to try once again to see Napoleon and then go home and tell his family that we're to be married. Not now, but in a few months, as there are certain business affairs to be taken care of first. Furthermore, his family has had no cause whatever to think of his remarrying, so he is not certain how they will receive the news."

Dominique looked off for a moment, murmuring with irony, "No, indeed, my dear, you must not have been in the least certain!" then looked down again and continued to read.

"Before we separated for the night, K asked us to promise him faithfully that we will never under any circumstances confide to anyone that he has been here. In one of Papa's usual dramatic gestures, he picked up the big family Bible, put it on the table, and swore— and so, of course, we all did, with a flourish, I can tell you! Half-laughing, we were, and yet there was a somberness in K's face that made my heart turn, as if he did not know what the future might bring to a doubter, a critic of the regime, and he wanted us safe. Our laughter covered our anxiety, I think. K himself seems not to be frightened, and yet I have detected in his expression at times that same sadness I felt in him when I first discovered how I loved him that day in the *petit-duc*. Perhaps only one who loves him as I do could have detected that sadness. But I will not be frightened. Surely—surely—but, no, I will not say it. He must come back. He must—he must."

14 DECEMBER 1804

"We have the news. Papa wants me to marry Carondel. It makes no difference. My life is finished. I can write no more."

Dominique looked up, sighed, leaned away from Nina, separated herself and sat motionless, sunk in her own silence. And then, "So that was the end. *Pauvre p'tite*," she said in a low voice. "*Ma pauvre Odile*."

"Domi," said Nina after a little, "Mrs. Staynes told me it's been years since she's read Odile's journal. If I could get her to read it again and she would put dates together, the dates of happenings she knows of in connection with your father's comings and goings, and the dates Odile speaks of—the length of time your father was away from the château at the end when no one knew where he was, the date K arrived at the Chrysostomes and then left, and the date he was shot in Paris —how could she help but see that K was your father? But most of all, I should think she would put their natures—their—"

"Characters?"

"Yes, their characters together. I can't tell her that K stands for Kot—"

"No. And I'm certain Kot would mean nothing to

[153]

her. As I said, it was an extremely private name and I doubt she could have come across it. But even if she would believe it was my father Odile loved, even then, what final proof is there, some proof that no one could deny, that Antoine de Lombre was the K of Odile's journal? There is only one thing that remains—"

"The painting, Domi? The one Chrysostome did of Kot and Odile?"

"Yes, the painting. And where is it? Not in this museum, though it might be in any one of dozens of others."

"But I don't understand," Nina said. "Surely Mrs. Staynes would know of it no matter where it is—"

"Which means only one thing," said Dominique. "That it has either been destroyed or lost track of. And I think most likely destroyed, by Chrysostome himself out of fear, out of concern for his family, so that no one would ever learn that K had been there. Oh, yes," said Dominique, "I'll wager that painting has been destroyed."

Chapter Sixteen

In Archy Archipenko's department, which was preserving and restoring, Nina was telling her parents, there was an Egyptian plate the museum had supposed was priceless, but that, under the X-ray, Mr. Archipenko had found to be a mass of tiny fragments all exquisitely fitted together and painted over. "A work of art—in a way," Archy had said, "but not, of course, priceless." A ninth-century Buddha he had found to be full of modern nails and screws and wires, and an ancient Tibetan wooden camel, supposedly whole, was shown to have a heavy metal pin in one leg. Lately he had been working on a medieval wooden statue whose face had had a split like a wound right down the front of it, which by steaming and very gentle, steady pressure, he had brought together again. He had healed the wound.

Nina saw, as she spoke of him, his round high-cheekboned face with its full mustache, its little eyes full of interest and enthusiasm as he explained his work to her. She saw the airy, white-painted room, full of light. On one of the deep windowsills were flowers he had brought from home, contrasting oddly with the laboratory-like atmosphere of the place: the fume cabinet, the cleaning tank for bathing statuary, the metal disinfecting cabinet that destroyed worms and insects, the oven where bronzes were dried to protect them from bronze disease, the workbench lined with lacquers and enamels and laid out with all gradations of brushes, the electron microscope, the air-abrasive which, with great skill and delicacy, removed varnish from paint, and dirt from stone statuary.

It was all fascinating to Nina. But was it to them —to her mother and father? In sudden bursts of remembering she was trying to pour it all out to both of them at once, her mother getting dinner in the kitchen and her father over on the couch near the fireplace, how it had been on her first day for "a recruit planning to make her career in a museum," Helena Staynes had said to Archy, "and very possibly," she added, "in this one."

"Mrs. Staynes took all that trouble over you, Nina," mused Mrs. Harmsworth in wonderment, "taking you around to meet everybody, and who knows what you'll do after college."

"Well, *I* know what I'm going to do," said Nina. She looked over at her father. Had he been listening, even? He had something on his mind, seeming removed, sitting there with his brooding, melancholy expression. While Nina set the table and fixed the salads roundabout her mother, he sat in front of the little flickering fire (their wood supply had come down from Silverspring along with the furniture) with his newspaper in his lap, looking at the flames or lifting his head when the mournful braying of the foghorn sounded over the water and the islands and the steep streets of the city. For the day had turned foggy toward late afternoon and now the gray billows were rolling in so that the lights down there were being gradually obscured as though a ghostly sea were drowning them. She had looked forward to sitting here at dinner watching the bright, intricate patterns, but nothing could spoil her pleasure, nothing dilute her pride and satisfaction in their new home.

"Mother, do you regret it now—our coming up here, the money it cost to move? Are you happy, darling?" She went up behind her mother and put her arms around her, confining for an instant the unceasing busyness. Then, without waiting for an answer, she went to one of the two windows at the end of the living room where they had put the dining table exactly as she had seen it on the day she had first come up. In the past, she thought, I pictured how everything would be in the future, and now the past and the future have come together to make the present. And so she thought of Domi and Gil, but did not trouble to tell herself why. "It's so *beau*tiful!" she said fervently, almost unbelievingly, looking out. And Mrs. Harmsworth all at once stopped her rattling of pots and the stirring of something and was silent, so that she must have been looking out of the long low window over the sink where the eaves came down. "Yes," she said, "yes, it *is* beautiful, Nina. And good to be able to look down and over, the way we used to in Silverspring, instead of being shut in a dark box."

"D'you remember our views, Nan?" spoke up Mr.

[157]

Harmsworth. It was the first remark he'd made since before Nina had begun her telling. "Do you still love the hills—do you remember the walks we used to take?"

Mrs. Harmsworth was going on with her stirring. "Of course, Chris," she said presently. "How could I forget? Why would I? It's only been six months. You make it sound years. But we have to catch up and there's no use talking about remembering."

"Do you ever think about going back up again—about going home?"

"Going home!" she repeated sharply. "*Going home!* What would be the sense of that? We've got something to do here in this city, so why would I waste my time thinking about going home?"

"I do," said Chris Harmsworth under his breath. "*I* do."

Nina turned to him, searched his face, and then went and knelt beside him.

"Dad. *Now?* Just when I'm beginning—"

"Oh, don't worry, Squirrel. I'm not planning anything. How can I? And apparently it's not up to me." He put out a finger and ran it down her forehead, down the bridge of her nose, her lips, and her chin. "Isn't it funny," he said, "how we've changed, you and I? Once it was you who was sick to go home." He made a little ironical sound in his throat that might have been the beginning of a laugh, and Nina leaned forward and laid her head against his chest and heard his heart beating, the slow, solid thud. Strange. Yes, it was—strange, strange!

"Now come away from mooning at the window,

Nina," called her mother. "Have you put the butter on, and the napkins? You always forget."

"Mother, Mrs. Staynes gave me her manuscript at the museum this morning." It was the only thing that had happened that had to do with Domi. Mrs. Staynes knew of no little name, no pet name, Antoine de Lombre had had. She knew of no painting Chrysostome had done of his daughter other than when she was a child or after her marriage. And she seemed not much interested in going back to Odile's journal just at present.

"Gave you her manuscript?" asked Chris Harmsworth with interest. "What do you mean *gave*, Squirrel?"

"Why, to read. And I want you to read it, too, Dad. When the mail came today, there was a box with her manuscript in it, and a letter, and after she read the letter her voice shook when she was talking to Jay Jacobs. He's the curator of decorative arts, and I like him. He's young, but I think they must have known each other for a long time because she didn't seem to mind crying in front of him. At least I think she was, though I couldn't see her face, and he tried to comfort her. He said he thought it was a fine piece of scholarly work and she said that was probably the trouble, that it was too damned scholarly, like a thesis. I don't know what that is. And then she said she must begin all over again, after all this time, and then Jay Jacobs went out and after a while, when I'd finished filing the costume plates and had to find out the next thing to do, I asked if I could read the carbon and she said that it would be a bore for me, that I was too young, but that if I was going to read it at all, she wanted me to have the original. And I'm going to start tonight."

Sometimes, at the museum, Domi would come and speak into Nina's ear at the most unexpected moments. One day at noon Nina was standing in front of a painting of the lake near the château, and Domi said, "See that ripple down there? That's the little snake that used to swim across from shore to shore, its tiny chin just ruffling the water. Chrysostome put him in the painting for fun because my father, when we went for walks, always watched for him. On the other side of the lake there was a marsh, a swampy place where bullrushes grew in their rough, velvety brown coats like rat's fur. The rushes were cut down every year and plaited into mats and rush carpets for the servants' bedrooms, and they always had to be damp before the plaiting. Marthe's bedroom, when I grew older and we each had our own instead of the nursery, never had any but a rush carpet spread over the cold red tiles, and no other scent, which I always thought the sweetest in the world and I wanted a carpet just like it for my own bedroom."

It was Domi who led Nina into a picture of an old parchment-colored book leaning against a large, dark metal object with a lid and a handle, a vase of branches flaming with yellow and orange and scarlet leaves, and a hand putting a long-stemmed pipe on the table near the book. The hand was Kot's, Domi said, a thin, strong-looking hand which, by the way it held the pipe, gave the feeling that it loved the textures of things. The book was the one he had treasured and read again and again as a little boy, scattered with the flower heads Domi had pressed in its pages that sent forth a breath full of witches' spells; the very book old Marthe had been reading when the news came that her master had been shot. The big dark object was Domi's footwarmer. Everyone had one, the cook, the sewing woman, the maids, Marie-Laure and Kot, each had his own, made of wrought iron, heavy, indestructible, one of the chief necessities of winter. "What a comfort they were!" said Domi. "We carried our footwarmers wherever we went, from fireplace to fireplace. I loved summer, the fierce Burgundian summers, when the cherries were almost honeyed by the heat and peach juice ran down our hands and chins and I would lie and watch the lizards, their little hides brilliant as if painted with green or blue or red enamel, doing their exercises—"

"Their push-ups," said Nina, remembering with a twist of longing their hot summer garden at Silverspring.

"Yes—yes," laughed Domi, "their push-ups, on the stone walls, and the goshawks would try to catch them and later the goshawks themselves would be caught and their speckled feathers used for our quilts.

"Long after all of us were gone from the château, I and my descendants—I died giving birth to my third child, did I ever tell you, Nina?—I used to wander through our deserted rooms, never lived in by my great-grandson, the one who sold our house to that family who modernized it, and our furniture and the paneling to Mrs. Staynes. By then, rubbish filled the courtyard where the stone children stood. A tangle of plant life covered everything. Animals had made their lairs among the brambles and when my descendant came

[161]

to open the château again to put it up for sale, he could scarcely push past the library doors that led into tunnels of greenery all rustling with birds and rabbits and squirrels.

"My father's heart would have ached to have seen the state of our house then, and how the fields and vineyards had been left to go to ruin and no one working the land anymore. He always loved the ritual necessities of the seasons, the harvesting of the wheat and the grapes, and then the wine-making. For him, his land was never separate from himself: one was a part of the other. Not even Chrysostome, an artist, was more aware of the natural world than my father. He said such strange things sometimes. One night he and my mother and I were standing out on the dark terrace looking up at the star-filled sky, and he said, 'Perhaps it comes from the farthest star, perhaps it is only a mouse running in the grass, but sometimes a whisper of sound catches me at my very center and all of existence opens up before me filled with a serene grandeur. I am not really afraid to die because I am one with the life around me.' And once he said that he felt such a difference between time in Paris, where it harried him mercilessly and there was never enough of it, and time in our own village where the slow passage of the days lifted him along easily and naturally so that he woke each morning refreshed, feeling that he could do all that he had to do."

"Domi," said Nina after a little, "if only Mrs. Staynes could be told everything you have ever told me about your father and that Odile has written about him. There's nothing like it in her book—nothing! She doesn't even begin to know him."

Chapter Seventeen

"The man she has portrayed is like a deserted house," Mr. Harmsworth said when he had finished the manuscript at the end of the week. And when Nina woke Monday morning, remembering what Domi had felt about the rooms in the museum, rooms that had once been her home, she knew what, just possibly, she could say to Mrs. Staynes. That is, she knew the words but not how to put them, and her hands were cold when she laid the manuscript in its box on Mrs. Staynes's desk. Most likely, she thought, she would not be asked to say anything at all. But Mrs. Staynes was looking at her, and,

"Did you read it, Nina?" she asked. "Or try to? Not for you, was it?"

"No, Mrs. Staynes, not for me. You were right, I'm too young for it. It's full of facts, and of course ideas, my father said."

"He read it, then?"

"Yes. He likes biography. He's read a good many."

"And he said—?"

"Do you mean you want me to tell you exactly what he said?"

"Exactly." And when Nina had repeated her father's words, Mrs. Staynes leaned back in her chair and folded her hands in her lap while she thought this over. "A deserted house," she said. "Cold and dark and silent. Now *there* is something to think about! No one has had the courage or the insight to tell me that."

"Mrs. Staynes, I thought of something in bed this morning. You saw the château in France. You saw it all run-down, but you could imagine, couldn't you, what it would have been like with Domi—Dominique— and Marie-Laure and Domi's father living there, and Marthe and old Maurice and Lisabetta and everybody, with all their personal possessions lying around?"

"I did, Nina. I did just that."

"And could you imagine, then, how someone would feel, someone who'd once lived there, coming here to the museum without knowing all that had happened in between and seeing the family furniture put around for people to look at instead of to live with, and none of the little things on the desks and tables and chairs, no books or sewing or papers or flowers? No family treasures in their own places, but all of them lined up in the wall cases with labels on them? It would be as if you were in a dream—your home and yet not your home. You would recognize everything, and yet not, in a way, because all the life would be gone. Perhaps that's what my father meant. And from being in the rooms here so much, imagining, and looking at the paintings of Maurice and Marthe and everybody, the one of Domi's father's pipe and that old book that I see

[164]

in so many backgrounds in the still lifes—so I suppose the family loved it—and the pictures of Domi with Lisabetta, and Domi and her parents, I thought there might be chapters in your book about all of them, and how they lived together and how their home life was, and the gardens, and what they talked about among themselves and how Domi and her father felt about each other and how her father felt when Marie-Laure died. You just put that she died in childbirth when Domi was twelve, nothing but a fact, but it seems to me, from the way they look in the paintings, that they must have been very happy together." Nina stopped. "It's so hard to express what I mean. I had it all thought out and *now* I haven't said it the way I wanted."

"But I understand what you mean, Nina. I do indeed. Yet as I did my reading, you see, as I did my research, these weren't just the things I was hunting for."

"But couldn't they have been a part?" Mrs. Staynes was silent. "I'm sorry," Nina said. "My mother thought it wouldn't help if I said anything, because most likely it would be impossible for me to say the right thing. For somebody my age to. And you're angry—"

"No, no, Nina, not angry at all." Mrs. Staynes got up abruptly and took the manuscript over and put it on the top shelf of the coat closet. "Do you remember asking me if there's a painting anywhere of Odile as a young woman, and my telling you that there's one of her at the Threlkeld house after her marriage? Mrs. Threlkeld called last night and I'm going there today to evaluate more of her things. She has all sorts of French objects of art she's willed to the museum as well as the Chrysostome of Odile and I thought you'd like to come along this afternoon and see it. Gil's here in the library going on with his interminable project—I've never known such a boy—and I thought we'd have lunch together down at Auguste's and then Gil could come with us. He said he'd like to."

Auguste, having finished eating, was sitting in his big chair smoking his pipe and had Lisabetta in his lap; he was stroking her and scratching her under the chin to make her bring her whiskers forward in the comical way cats have. And sometimes he'd give her little firm taps on her skull between the ears—pok, pok, pok—with his first finger, and with closed eyes she would lift her head as if this sensation too she found rapturous for some unguessable cat reason. Nina was sitting on the floor at Auguste's feet waiting for Gil and Mrs. Staynes to finish lunch when, watching Lisabetta, she saw the cat's eyes open suddenly, the black pupils widen from slits to circles as they would do in darkness, and then Lisabetta's head turn as though following some quick movement. And when Nina twisted round to discover what Lisabetta was looking at, there was Domi's Lisabetta, seeming the ghost of her pale ghost self in a shaft of brilliant sunlight slanting in at the open doorway, but her colors deepening, appearing to take on substance as she left the shaft of light and whirled in a circle, chasing her own tail. "Oh, Lisabetta!" Nina laughed, unthinking, and clapped in delight to watch the lithe body twisting and doubling, the tabby paws coming together over her own gray tail, the tail escaping as though it had a will of its own, and the chase continue. Now Auguste's Lisabetta, unable to endure that the other should be enjoying herself all alone, flashed from his lap and the two cats leaped at one another, passed through each other's bodies, rolled and batted, hissing, growling in mock fury, then darted back from one another, bellies flattened to the floor, heads tilting from side to side in quick, coy, nervous excitement.

"Why, Lisabetta!" cried Helena Staynes in astonishment. "Whatever possesses you!"

Auguste chuckled. "That's it! That's it! Whatever possesses! That is what I ask myself. *Soudainement*, away she go, out there when I work an' she sit an' watch close by, the way she like to do. *Soudainement*, she see something I don' see an' off she tear, as if she 'ave a frien'—some special frien'."

Now Lisabetta, Auguste's Lisabetta, shot over Nina's lap, whisked up the arm of Auguste's chair, along the back of it, and down and off over the floor and out the door, and Domi's Lisabetta in wild pursuit, swept through Nina's hands, held out to catch that swift shape that seemed no more ghostly to Nina now than the other Lisabetta. Wholly absorbed in the chase, she watched Domi's cat swerve in a twinkling and take off after her companion and disappear from sight. From my sight, occurred to Nina in the next breath. From *my* sight only. Lost in her own pleasure, she had entirely forgotten Auguste and Helena Staynes and Gil, and now her eyes flew to them, but Mrs. Staynes was still watching Auguste's Lisabetta through the open doorway, and Auguste was tapping out his pipe ready to get up and start back to work.

Only Gil was watching her. And when their eyes met, he gave her a curious little quick smile, looked down again and crushed up his lunch papers, then Mrs. Staynes's, and stood up and said, "Let's go."

Mrs. Threlkeld, Helena Staynes had told Nina, was ninety, and so this firm, busty woman who answered the door with a copper watering can in one hand could not have been the old lady—more likely the housekeeper, Nina thought. And then as she and Mrs. Staynes and Gil stepped into the hall, Nina's whole attention was centered upon the little creature coming forward to meet them, tiny, bent, nothing but a handful of bones, she seemed, with a white face fined down to its basic structure, the fragile flesh stretched over cheekbones and jaw, but lighted by large gray eyes set in sooty sockets. Her white hair, the few feathers of it, was brushed up into a topknot supported by a strip of tangerine ribbon, which gave her a jaunty air. She had on a long gray silk dress, and she must have been habitually cold for, despite the warmth of the house, she was wrapped in a black woolen shawl. She came toward them slowly, her hands, like shells, held tremblingly out to Nina, and Nina took them in her own large, warm, enveloping ones.

"Oh, how good!" cried a wisp of voice, faint and high. "How good that feels! Child, I wish you could hold my hands forever—" and the little woman started to laugh, a small screech. "So cold," she said when she could get her breath. "Always so cold. Poor Bertha Moffatt here says I'll be the death of her." Again the sharp little screech. "Well, we'll see who makes it first—Bertha or me. Now, you're Nina, the one who wants to see my Odile. Run along upstairs, children, run along. Look at anything you like—anything at all. And Bertha and Helena and I will go in here and have some nice hot tea." She smiled and nodded, then turned on Helena Staynes's arm into what must have been "the drawing room," thought Nina, where she saw the tea things already laid out and then she and Gil moved toward the stairs on their right. As she started up, for the first time she became aware of her surroundings.

She was in a long, narrow hall that had a high ceiling. The woodwork was white and the walls were covered with an old-fashioned but very handsome moss-green and white-figured wallpaper. There was a dark green rug on the floor—a silky rug like Mam'zelle's, silky and thick—that went up the stairs. To the side of the stairway on her right there was an enormous window reaching up two stories that let in a broad fall of sunlight. There were ferns and all sorts of flowering plants grouped thickly in a brass planter along the base of the broad windowsill. The fragrance of flowers, the fresh, damp smell of ferns and of watered earth was in her nostrils. Her feet sank into the softness of the carpet. She noted how its pile shone in the leaf-caught, moving patches of sunlight, how immaculately rich and smooth was the enamel on the spools of the banisters. And she could hear Helena Staynes speaking, her voice wandering off down there in the room on the left side of the hall. And it was Gil who was at her elbow.

Ever since the night she had first had dinner at Gil's and she'd told the Patricks her dream, she had asked herself who it could have been standing unseen, a little behind her, just touching her elbow. Now she knew. The feathery chill she had always associated with Domi

[169]

rippled round the back of her neck and down her arms. She put her hand out to find his. "Here we are, Gil. Do you understand? Do you remember my dream of the high-ceilinged hall and the stairs? But where are the stone children? They were running up ahead of me, laughing, and when Odile got to the second floor, she went off and the others followed, calling to each other, but Odile said no, she wouldn't come until I'd seen something first, and she hung over the banister looking down at me and she was excited and telling me to come quick."

Nina turned and looked at Gil, and his face, even in the sunlight, seemed pale, or was it the reflection of greenness, of the rug and the ferns, that made him seem so? He passed his tongue over his lips. Their hands were still clasped. "It was the painting she wanted you to see, wasn't it?" he said. "It could only be that. But why was she excited? Let's go on up."

Chapter Eighteen

And when they came into the upper hall and turned the corner, there was Odile. Her face was radiant, her mouth open a little as if she were speaking, and she seemed on the verge of stepping right out of the full-length portrait, the tip of one shoe visible under the hem of her white dress. She had on a red cloak buttoned at the throat and one hand was up as if about to undo the buttons and toss the cloak aside. Her other was reaching back to take the outstretched hand of a man who stood slightly behind her, a man heavily built, considerably older than she, stout, smiling in self-satisfaction but with little eyes cool and shrewd in contrast to the comfortable rosiness of his face. There was a lantern on the floor at his feet and the hand that may just have put it down was now taking a pipe from his coat pocket. At the bottom of the painting, inscribed in a small plaque in the ornate gold frame were the words, *Madame Odile and Monsieur Hippolyte Calome Carondel.*

Nina stood in silence in front of the painting. Mrs. Staynes had said that no one knew that that stone figure in the courtyard was Odile as a child. And it was true that Odile had changed as she became a young woman—but I can see the stone child in the courtyard, Nina told herself. I can see that this is my Odile. And she could *never* have been happy with that man in the painting—never, never!

"So this is Carondel," she said.

"What do you think, Nina? Why did Odile want you to come up?"

"Because the painting is a lie. And she wanted me to see it's a lie. How could Chrysostome have done it, painted her that way with Carondel when it would have been impossible for her to have felt like that with him, looking as if this was the most perfect—" She stopped. "Gil, this is Odile with Kot, the one she called K in her journal, just the initial K. This is Odile after she'd come in from the barn with him when they'd told one another for the first time that they loved each other and he'd asked her to marry him. And when they came in and stood in the doorway together—see, Kot has just put down the lantern Odile took out with her—her father asked them to stay there at the door just as they were so that he could catch them, sketch them like that, and later Odile said that he made the sketch into a painting. I know this is it. I know! I mean I know that this is how it was meant to be, with Kot standing there instead. But Chrysostome must have got rid of that other painting after Kot was killed, because he was afraid, and then he painted this one with Odile in the same position and with her same look, because everyone agreed it was one of the best portraits he'd ever done."

"Unless," said Gil after a little silence, "unless

Chrysostome just painted over—what was his name?—Kot. Just painted over Kot and put Carondel in instead. That's the way it could have been. Because if the painting of Odile was so fine, he wouldn't have wanted to destroy it for fear he couldn't get her again the way he had the first time. He'd have to have caught her when she was happy, as happy as she'd been in that moment with Kot when they first came in. Then, what did you say happened?"

"They shot K—Napoleon's soldiers did. Napoleon thought he was subversive, and so it was made out that K had murdered his own valet, old Maurice, and they said they shot him for that. Afterwards Chrysostome wanted Odile to marry Carondel. But she didn't love him, Gil. She laughed at the very idea of marrying that old man."

"So then she would only have been happy like *this*," said Gil, "when K was alive. And there wouldn't have been any reason for Chrysostome to destroy one of the best portraits he'd ever done when he could just put Carondel in the place of K. Don't you see?"

Nina thought. "And yet how can it be proved that Kot is there, if he is, underneath Carondel? That's what's so hopeless—"

"But they can get at Kot under the painting of Carondel. If Mrs. Threlkeld would let the museum take the painting, Archy could make an X-ray, and if there's someone there underneath, it will show."

For Nina, everything came together into a pattern as though a kaleidoscope had turned. "I've got to go down and talk to them. And please don't say anything. You must not let the name Kot slip out, the way I've done with you. Mrs. Staynes only knows K from Odile's journal, but I know who he is and she would never be able to understand that."

Nina was about to turn away when Gil put his hand on her arm. "Nina," he said, "I saw you at Auguste's. I saw you reach out for what seemed to be nothing, and then I saw you look up at us and the expression on your face when you thought we might have seen. And I remember going over to the grotto that day Mam'zelle wanted you, and I thought somebody had been there, and you had the strangest look on your face. But you were alone. You seemed to be alone, and yet I felt you hadn't been. Really, I *knew* you hadn't. I've thought about that."

Nina looked at him, and then went to the head of the stairs. "I'm going to talk to them now. I'm going to ask them if the painting can be X-rayed, but I've got to think how to do it. I don't know how to begin."

In the drawing room, as Nina called it to herself because of its elegance, she and Gil were offered cake and coffee, which went down very comfortably, lunch having been all of an hour and a half ago. Nina listened to the others, wanting not to talk but to turn the whole matter over in her mind. And finally Mrs. Threlkeld, who was sitting in a low fireside chair at the end of the coffee table, finished telling Helena Staynes a story about the porcelain figure she held in her lap and then turned to Nina.

"Was the picture of Odile all you'd hoped, Nina? Mrs. Staynes says you have some special, very strong, personal feeling for her because of one of Chrysostome's stone children in the courtyard, which you seem to think is Odile, and because of a journal she wrote."

Nina put down her cup and saucer and plucked some crumbs from her lap and put them in her napkin. "Mrs. Threlkeld, have you ever read Odile's journal?"

The old lady blinked, looking away, trying to remember. "Now, I don't believe I have. At least I don't recall. Yet I've always been very much interested in anything to do with the Chrysostomes ever since I bought that painting up there almost fifty years ago."

"Mrs. Threlkeld, near the end of her journal Odile tells about coming in from the barn with a man she calls K, someone she'd loved ever since she was a child. And they've decided to get married, and her father asks them to stand right there at the door while he sketches them because they look so happy, and after that he made the sketch into a painting."

Mrs. Threlkeld waited for Nina to go on, but Helena Staynes suddenly leaned forward. "Nina, I don't understand. You can't possibly have read the end of the journal. The only copy of volume two in the museum is Mam'zelle's, and that's in French."

Nina held her breath and looked down.

"Now, that's a strange thing, isn't it?" she said after a little. "But still, Mam'zelle and I talked a lot about the whole journal."

"Oh, I see. Yes, I suppose you did." Now Helena Staynes seemed to dismiss this small detail from her mind. "But I don't understand what all that about Chrysostome sketching K and Odile at the door has to do with the painting upstairs."

"You *don't?* But the painting up there is the one Odile was talking about! I'm sure it is! I think that K

is there under Carondel, because never, never could
she have had a look like that on her face holding out
her hand to bring in a fat old farmer. After loving K
the way she did? How *could* she! Why, she looks as if
she's ready to fly away with joy! Don't you *see* it,
Mrs. Staynes? Haven't you ever thought about that?"

Helena Staynes was looking at Nina now as she had
in her office when they were talking about the manuscript. "No, Nina," she said in a low voice, "no, I'll
have to confess I never have. But then I first read
Odile's journal in France about fourteen or fifteen years
ago right after it was published, and I saw the painting
upstairs for the first time only a few years ago. I've
never put the two together. I've really forgotten a great
deal about the journal."

All at once Mrs. Threlkeld rose up on her little
stick legs and stood there with her arms out as if she
were about to swim away or perhaps go wading. "Help
me, please, Bertha," she said. "I want to go up in the
elevator and have a look. And I will tell you one thing,"
she said, as Bertha Moffatt went to her and put an arm
around her waist, "I will tell you this. I have stood
many times and looked at that picture and I have always
thought that the likeness of Carondel—the artistry of
the brushwork, I mean—to be much inferior to that in
the face and figure of Odile. And I have never understood this. Some who have looked at it can detect no
difference, but then *they* haven't lived with it. I could
only say to myself that possibly Chrysostome wasn't
much inerested in Carondel, while we can easily imagine
how he felt about Odile. But, child, if the man she

loved *is* under there, then we can understand both Odile's expression and just possibly the difference in the way those two figures are painted. Come, let's go up! I'm tingling inside myself—"

Upstairs Nina heard the glide of a metal door opening and closing, and then Bertha Moffatt emerged at the far end of the hall with Mrs. Threlkeld and they came slowly along. They all looked at the painting.

"Do you see what I mean, Helena—the difference between the artistry of Odile and of Carondel?"

"I'm not sure I do—"

"Nevertheless it must be X-rayed. I *want* it X-rayed!" said Mrs. Threlkeld, "And as soon as possible. Call Jay Jacobs, Helena, and have him come at once and pack it up."

"However," said Bertha Moffatt, "there's the insurance."

"I'll call the insurance company immediately I get back," Helena Staynes said, "and have them write up the papers, and as soon as Jay can get them, he and Bill Gunderby will come for the painting—probably tomorrow."

"Blazes!" said Mrs. Threlkeld. "I forgot the insurance. *Drat* the insurance." Then Nina felt a touch on her hand. "Child, what can you be thinking?" Nina had been aware of nothing but her own thoughts since the words, "Nevertheless it must be X-rayed. I *want* it X-rayed—" and she did not answer. "Yes, it's rather incredible, isn't it, Nina? So much to happen because you put the journal and the painting together. Is that what you're thinking?"

"No," said Nina. "No, Mrs. Threlkeld. I'm thinking how happy Domi will—I mean, how happy Domi *would* be."

There was a little silence, and then, "But I don't see, Nina," said Helena Staynes, "what Dominique has to do with it."

Nina considered. "That was a slip of the tongue, wasn't it? I should have said, 'how happy Odile would be.' "

Around five, Nina was alone in the registration office typing cards very slowly and carefully for the inventory file. She had Mrs. Staynes's notes for each object that had recently been acquired by the museum, and Mrs. Staynes, before Jay Jacobs and Mam'zelle came in, had been explaining them to her.

First you put the object's entire number, Helena Staynes said, which is made up of the year it was acquired, how many there are of that kind of object in the museum, the number of this object within its particular collection, and the number of parts the object has. After that, you put whether it is a gift, a purchase, a bequest, or an exchange; then the value of the object; the name and address of the donor, or of the person who has willed it to the museum, or of the agent in case the object is an exchange; then a description of the object—

"But I've never known anything *like* it," Mrs. Staynes exclaimed suddenly, as if her thoughts had been running like water under the dry facts of acquisition, "your feeling for someone like Dominique, Nina, the power of your imagination! Have you always been like this, imagining, as though they actually exist, certain people you read or hear about? No, but it's more than this, more than simply imagining! To you, Odile, and even more intensely, it seems to me, Dominique de Lombre *exist*. You always call her Domi, as if you know her personally. And perhaps her father, too, to the point where my book never for a moment increased your sense of his reality but bitterly disappointed it and fell so far short that you were almost desperate as to how to make me see this without hurting my feelings. At Mrs. Threlkeld's you wanted to say, 'I'm thinking how happy Domi will be,' then caught yourself and said 'would.' But I think you meant 'will.' And it's quite possible you meant Odile, but somehow I felt not. Dominique was the person you had in mind. What is it, Nina? What has happened? What has the museum done to you?"

Nina had no idea what to say. "It's only," she began slowly, "that I'd never seen a building like this. I love where we used to live up in the hills looking out at the mountains. But it's the outdoors that's beautiful there. Even though we were happy in it, our house was ordinary. It was just a house, not very big. And all the houses up there are the same, and our little museum is an old store made over into a National Monument. That's kind of funny in a way, I guess, but I didn't think so. I'd never known any place like this, a real museum with paintings like Chrysostome's and *Time Is a River Without Banks* and with long wide halls and big windows at the end where you look out onto lawns and gardens, and with a courtyard and stone children, and shining floors and paneling and rooms with furniture that belonged all that time ago to the people in the paintings."

Mrs. Staynes was silent, and Nina looked up and saw those striking, deep-set eyes studying her with both warmth and mystification. "I wonder," Helena Staynes said presently, "if that can really be all, Nina. And if you *did* say 'Domi' unconsciously, because it was actually she you were thinking of, I wonder why Dominique would be happy that the painting is to be X-rayed." She waited, but Nina did not answer, because there was no answer that could be given, and after a little Mrs. Staynes took up the pencil she had tossed down. "Where were we?" she said. "Oh, yes, a description of the object—"

And then Mam'zelle and Jay Jacobs came in and had to be told the whole story of Mrs. Threlkeld's painting, and the questions Nina had asked and what, because of them, was to be done with it. And after they had gone out with Mrs. Staynes and she was left alone, Nina was too excited to go on typing, considering the things they had said about her. She kept making mistakes and presently she felt that Domi was there.

"Domi?"

"Yes, Nina." Dominique was standing by the window, scarcely visible at first, but as Nina continued to look at her, seeming to become more substantial, to take on color and form.

"Did you hear everything, Domi? Do you understand that when Mrs. Staynes sees the X-ray she will know that she must completely rewrite the end of her book?"

"Not just the end of it, Nina. *The whole thing*."

Now Domi came closer and stood there at the side of the desk and gave an excited little laugh. "Let me see you work that object," she said. "That preposterous looking object. How the air is full of hard noises in your time: the clacking you make with your fingers, and bells ringing on those things you speak into, and the mowing machines of Auguste and Philippe and those machines that whine like hurt animals that the cleaning women use when the museum is closed and everything is swept and dusted and polished and finger-prints wiped off the glass of the cases. And the cries of those hard, shiny carriages in the street, and the throbbing in the sky of enormous silver-colored birds that sometimes let out a fearful tearing sound when they go so fast I can only rarely see them pass over, a sound like a gigantic piece of silk being ripped. I don't understand, Nina, why sounds are getting harder and louder. I loved the whisper of my father's pen scurrying over the paper, and I loved the hushing sound of the gardeners' brooms when I first woke in the morning and all the different sounds of horses' hooves. Yes, but there were clods of peasants then who beat their horses, and some never gave them enough to eat and some over-worked them. Now that, at least, is over. *Merci le bon Dieu!* Nina, we don't yet know anything at all about the painting. No one can be certain whose face is under Carondel's. Perhaps no face—only canvas."

Chapter Nineteen

As it turned out, both Jay Jacobs and Mr. Gunderby, the director of displays, were busy the next day working on the setting up of an exhibit of tureens, which was scheduled to open the following morning. "Soup pots!" cried Mrs. Threlkeld, when this was explained to her. "Does anybody really care about those things?"

But at three o'clock they were finished and Jay and Bill Gunderby took the insurance papers over to the old lady's house and got the painting. By five-thirty Mam'zelle and Helena Staynes and Jay and Nina and Gil were in Archy Archipenko's department and Archy had the painting under the X-ray. A few minutes later he brought out a large negative of that portion of the painting that contained the head and shoulders of Carondel. Now he slipped it into the lighted viewing box, and there indeed was a face looking out at them through the faintly visible features of the farmer, but whose face it was could not be determined. It would not take him too long, Archy said, to get a print, and when he had brought them the developed photograph and laid it on the table,

"Why, Helena, that's Antoine de Lombre!" exclaimed Jay incredulously.

Helena Staynes only stared at the face she knew so well, of whom there were three portraits in the Chrysostome gallery. She was plainly unable to speak.

"It *is*, Jay," said Mam'zelle. "It *is*. But I don't understand, because as I remember, the K of Odile's journal—the K she was going to marry—was a young man by the name of Julien Korin. At least so everyone thought at the time the journal was published."

"But K was *not* Julien Korin," said Mrs. Staynes softly. "He was de Lombre. And so now I must read Odile's journal all over again, from beginning to end. And because I know that K *was* Antoine de Lombre, I will discover a whole world of knowledge about him that I never dreamed existed. And that world will lead me to others. For instance, where is Chrysostome's journal? Because it seems to me, now that I think of it, that Odile started keeping hers because her father had one. Nina!" and her eyes turned from the photograph and came up to rest on Nina's. "You said—I remember you saying something at Mrs. Threlkeld's about how happy Dominique would be. But how could you know?"

Nina looked at her, and then away. "It was a slip of the tongue. You remember I told you—"

Now the rest of them went on talking, while Nina continued to feel Helena Staynes's eyes asking their question which could not be answered. And in a little,

Archy, who had left the room immediately after the discovery of Antoine de Lombre's face lying there beneath Carondel's, came back again.

"Helena," he said, "did de Lombre have any sort of nickname?"

"None that I ever discovered."

"Well, look at this, then." And he put another photograph over the first. "I took this at the bottom of the back of the painting." Through the title, *Madame Odile and Monsieur Hippolyte Calome Carondel*, which Chrysostome had written on the back in black paint, were now visible the words, *Odile and Kot, betrothed December 3, 1804*.

There was a rather long silence. And then, "The work you've given me, Nina!" said Helena Staynes finally. "All to be done over, hasn't it! All to be written over again—the entire book. But I see it. I see the whole thing. I *feel* it, and I think I know now just about how it's got to be done."

Chapter Twenty

On this cold, blowy evening in the middle of July,
Auguste had a fire going in the big fireplace and Lisabetta was stretched on the hearth blinking at the
flames. Everyone was gathered around the long table.
Mam'zelle was at one end and Auguste, as host, was at
the other. Nina, Jay Jacobs, Mr. Quarles, Helena
Staynes, Mr. and Mrs. Harmsworth, Mrs. Threlkeld and
Bertha Moffatt, Gil and his mother and father, Archy
Archipenko, Edna Kendrick, Mr. Gunderby and his
helper, Nils, and the three museum secretaries, Rose
and Phyllis and Jinny, were ranged around in between,
up one side of the table and down the other, twenty in
all. Philippe was away on vacation.

Auguste and Mam'zelle had prepared the meal—
a meal, Dr. Patrick declared, fit for gourmets: the onion
soup for which Auguste had been making the stock for
days, his tossed salad, his flaky croissants, five legs of
lamb rubbed with garlic, lemon juice, mustard, curry
and marjoram, and basted with wine and currant jelly,
and then the dessert of fruit compote with Mam'zelle's

special sauce poured over. At the beginning they had all toasted Nina with a champagne Mam'zelle had had stored away in her "cellar," which was the wine closet in her apartment, and at the end, Dr. Patrick proposed a toast to Mam'zelle and Auguste for the artistry of their cooking.

"Now, Nina," said Gil, "tell them about your dream of going upstairs at Mrs. Threlkeld's. This is the time to tell it."

She hadn't known in her dream, she said, who was coming up behind her, and had mentioned this in telling Gil and his parents the whole dream several weeks ago. Now she told of Gil being asked at the last minute to go to Mrs. Threlkeld's with Mrs. Staynes and herself, of the two of them starting up the stairs together and the truth dawning on her just as she had her foot on the first step that this was her dream, and then turning and understanding who it was who had been there at her elbow in her dream, and of how Gil, in that same instant, had realized what was happening—that they were both, now, in the midst of the dream's becoming a reality. When she had finished her telling,

"But who are the stone children, Nina?" asked her mother.

"The children at the museum—in the courtyard. Odile and her brothers and sisters."

"And Odile, apparently, in your dream, was wanting you to go up because of the painting?"

"Yes. Why else would she have been so excited? She wanted me to find out the truth—that Carondel didn't belong beside her."

"But it's so strange and unheard of that it makes me go cold all over—"

"Yet thousands of people have had prophetic dreams, Mrs. Harmsworth," said Gil. "Lincoln had one just before he was shot that foretold his death. In it he heard people crying and someone said to him, 'The President has been assassinated.'"

"But, Nina," said Mrs. Threlkeld, her eyes shining in their dark sockets, "do you mean that you saw my house in your dream, the hall exactly as it is in every detail, before you were ever aware that it existed, before Mrs. Staynes had told you anything about me?"

"Yes, in every detail—the high ceiling, the wallpaper, the color of the rug, the way the stairs curve, the big window going up two stories with the planter at the bottom filled with ferns and flowers. And here's a strange thing: in my dream the earth smelled damp. And when Mrs. Staynes and Gil and I came to your house, Miss Moffatt answered the door with a watering can in her hand, and when I went up the stairs, the earth in the planter smelled damp."

"It was," said Bertha Moffatt.

"You mean, you didn't know beforehand, before the dream," said Dr. Patrick, "that you were soon to see the painting of Odile?"

"I didn't even know such a thing existed, let alone where it was. My dream came long before I asked Mrs. Staynes if there was a painting of Odile grown up."

"But Nina's prophetic dream," said Mrs. Kendrick, "is no stranger than life itself—or the curious workings of time."

"But prophetic dreams and the curious workings of time go together," said Gil. "Prophetic dreams mean that all time—past, present, and future—is one Time. How can it not be, if the dream knows to the last detail exactly what is going to happen? Actually, the happening isn't *going* to happen. It *Is*."

"It's as if," said Jay Jacobs, "we're ants walking on a tapestry already woven, and having no idea of the whole design but only of the little part we're standing on—"

"That's it!" exclaimed Gil, "that's it! Prophetic dreams would be impossible if the pattern, with all its complex weaving, weren't already there."

"And you, Dr. Patrick?" asked Helena Staynes, leaning forward. "What do you think?"

He smiled and looked away. "I'm a physicist," he said, "who takes delight in the Uncertainty Principle. There's a logic in Gil's argument, but somehow I'm convinced that in creation there's something strange in the proportion, something reasoning can never quite get at, and I hope it never will. Which shows what a traitor I am as a scientist."

Gil did not appear to have been listening. "Dad," he said in a low voice, "Dad, you know I've been thinking, and maybe the same thing bothers Mrs. Threlkeld. If I'm right, what's the use of struggling through a pattern already laid down?"

"No use," said his father, "unless we make a use."

Nina stood in the courtyard. Brilliant moonlight shone down into this small enclosed place of stone and greenery as though into a cup, and the water in the fountain, leaping and falling, caught the moonlight in its drops. The stone children stood with their hands out and the moonlight was reflected from the floor of the court-yard up into their faces. Or perhaps a face would be revealed in a fall of clear silver when the leaves over its head were blown aside, and the eyes, set in their shadowed caves, then appeared more subtly expressive than ever. As Nina went from one to another of the children, looking up at them, they seemed to her, far more so now than in the moving sun and shadow of daylight, to be magical: imbued with a secret, vibrant, and elusive life. *"Les images merveilleux,"* murmured Nina, though had she thought, she would not have been able to remember ever reading the words nor hearing them spoken.

Mam'zelle and Helena Staynes had taken Nina to Mam'zelle's office and there Mam'zelle had given her volume two of Odile's journal, "so that you can teach yourself French, Nina," she had said, "from a book that seems especially yours, just as the first part did." And as Nina took it and held it in her hand with the other poised to open it, it fell open of its own accord to the final page and Nina heard all at once Dominique's voice reading that last brief entry.

" *'Nous avons les nouvelles,'* " read Nina aloud, and knew herself to be echoing Domi's very tones, every curl of her tongue. " *'Papa désire que j'épouse Carondel. Ce ne fait rien. Ma vie est finie. Je ne peux plus écrire.'* " Then she looked up at Mam'zelle and Helena Staynes and there was a little pause before Mam'zelle spoke.

"No one, Nina," she said. "who has not lived in France could speak the language like that—lived in

France, and specifically somewhere in the Burgundian countryside. You have just now spoken as a native Burgundian, with those rich, rolling r's that hit the back of the throat in a certain, recognizable way. The accent is unmistakable."

Another silence, and then, "Dominique de Lombre was a Burgundian," said Helena Staynes.

Still Nina said nothing. She only looked at them.

"*C'est un mystère*, Nina," said Mam'zelle as she had once before. "*C'est un grand mystère*."

"And yet, perhaps not, Vicky," said Helena, "if what Gil believes is true. Perhaps not."

Now Nina went to Odile and put a hand on the smooth arm. "Call her, Odile. Call Domi." Nina had not seen Dominique for the past two weeks, and when the meaning of her absence at last swept over her, she had cried.

She waited, listening and watching. And in memory she suddenly saw Domi again as she had once before here in the courtyard, her arms up and her hair swinging down her back. "Look, Nina, look!" she called, and it was the sky she had meant. "The color of it—at this time of evening." "Venus, Domi," Nina had called back. "See up there? That's Venus—"

In this moment she was acutely aware of her own life enmeshed with that of the stone children, aware of a pervading joy that had its source she knew not where. And in the midst of her joy she saw minutely every object in the courtyard, standing there in the moonlight, intensely itself yet at the same time a part of her own being as if her whole body, each of her senses, were alive to every shift and tremor of stone and leaf and air. "*Domi*," she called aloud in the stillness, "*Domi, do you hear me? I'm ready. Let me come—*" Still with her arm around Odile, she held her body poised, willing herself over the brink, her breathing caught, in the concentration of her desire to follow Domi, without consciousness of need for breath, and her eyes opened to their widest while she waited for that moment when her angle of vision might be changed by the minutest degree and she could see Domi again.

But at length, quietly and finally, she knew that Domi was gone and would not come back, that there was no use waiting and calling. All the children were stone and The Moment had passed.

She stood for a little, leaning against Odile, listening to the murmur of the courtyard, the small sound of the fountain, the wind lifting the leaves. Then her arm slid down, and she turned, and went in.